Hall

Book One of The Cost of

Redemption Series

By

Mary Alford

COPYRIGHT FOR HALLOWED GROUND

Prologue

The dust and debris from the explosion mushroomed in all directions, covering everything within a quarter mile in an ash-gray veil. Agent Erin Sandoval couldn't see beyond her hand in front of her.

She'd lost visual of her partner in the confusion that ensued seconds before the explosion propelled her backwards some ten feet in the air. The building—a safe house—was destroyed. Reduced to a pile of rubble in seconds. No one in the belly of the structure could have survived the blast.

"Blake!" Erin yelled into the settling silence, breaking the first rule of an ambush. Never give your position away to the enemy.

The silty haze that settled over the area made it nearly impossible to see anything. Her voice sounded muffled. Disjointed. Frantic. She *was* frantic. Where was Blake?

Dear God, please let him be okay.

"What happened? Where is he?" Kabir, the team's Pakistani guide, materialized next to Erin, weapon drawn.

There was only one place Blake could be.

"He's in there." She threw the words over her shoulder as she ran for the carcass of the building. Before she'd covered more than a couple feet, someone grabbed both arms, holding her in place.

"Blake!" Relief threatened to take her legs out from under her. "You're safe." She whirled only to find it wasn't Blake at all. Jackson "Jax" Murphy, the commander of the Special Activities Division, the CIA's covert paramilitary-operations unit, held her in a vise grip.

Erin struggled to free herself from Jax's grasp. "Let me go. He's in there and he could be hurt."

Jax didn't relent. "You can't go in there. The building isn't secure."

She understood the danger. They'd all lost comrades to the war on terror. The insurgents had perfected the deadly "double threat," as it was known. If the first explosion didn't do the trick, the second one would. Still, she didn't care. This was Blake.

"We can't wait for help. He needs us," she insisted.

Jax didn't budge. "You don't know that for certain. Stand down, Erin. That's an order."

Out of the smoke and chaos, the marines attached to the mission appeared like a ghostly tribe. They were well trained in disarming this latest threat.

"Search the building. We have an agent missing." Jax's gaze held hers. "He could be injured."

The squad commander gave Jax a quick nod, then motioned for the team to enter the remains.

Jax finally released her. "What happened? How'd you two get separated?"

The sniper attack had taken both of them by surprise. Their intelligence had confirmed that the area was free of enemy insurgents' hours earlier. Obviously, that wasn't the case. The enemy had been expecting them. A firefight between Erin and Blake and possibly five rebel soldiers broke out, followed by the explosion.

"We were ambushed. They were waiting for us, Jax. Blake and I ducked behind that burned-out vehicle over there. Blake was with me until . . ."

He'd thrown away caution because he believed they were both sitting targets and he wanted to protect her. He made a break for it, determined to draw fire away from Erin. Before she could stop him, the explosion lit up the night and shook their world. The last visual she had of him was heading for the building.

"He's in there, I know it, and he needs me." She didn't wait for Jax to stop her. As she entered the building's remains, she met the first marine exiting. The truth was obvious in his grim expression.

"Please, no," Erin whispered. Keeping her panic at bay was impossible. The smoke hung thick in the air as she scanned the remains until she saw him lying on the dirt floor. Her partner since the day he'd recruited her. She'd completed her first tour of duty with the second invasion into Afghanistan at his side.

Three marines worked on defusing the second bomb. The rest of the unit knelt around the man who'd been like a brother to her. Agent Blake Robertson.

She covered her mouth with a trembling hand and fell to her knees beside him.

One of the two soldiers had balled up his jacket and held it against the wound to try and stop the bleeding in a futile effort. The jacket and everything around it was soaked in blood.

Why'd you do it? Tears blurred her vision. It wasn't supposed to end like this. "No," was all she could get to come out. She gently touched Blake's face. The vacant eyes staring into space would haunt her forever. "I'm sorry. I'm so sorry."

Someone knelt next to her. Jax. He'd been Blake's best friend for longer than Erin had known her partner.

Jax reached over and closed Blake's eyes. The finality of the gesture was too much. Erin covered her eyes with her hands and collapsed. She'd lost her best friend to a war that felt impossible to win. To a group of people bent on their destruction, filled with hate. Justified by what they believed was "the cause."

"We have to leave, Erin. Now. The marines can't defuse the bomb. There's something different about this one." Jax grabbed her arms and lifted her to her feet.

"No." She wouldn't leave Blake alone. Not like this.

"Now, Agent." Jax half-dragged, half-carried her toward the safe area that had been set up some distance from the building.

Her thoughts wouldn't come together no matter how hard she tried to make them. She couldn't focus. Blake's lifeless eyes were there before her wherever she looked. He'd died. She'd lived. Why?

"Don't stop. There's no time," Jax said when she turned to look back at Blake one last time. They were almost out of the ruins.

She barely had time to register the shock in Jax's voice when the world around them rumbled and shook, then exploded into hell on earth.

Chapter One

One month later . . .

"You know I love you, don't you, baby sister?"

She spun to see his face and laughed in spite of the sweltering heat of the day that stuck their clothes to their bodies. This had been a running joke between herself and Blake from the beginning. She was his sister, and he was her brother. They clicked that way.

Blake was just a big kid at heart. At thirty-five, he resembled a slightly taller, definitely more freckled version of Opie Taylor.

The day had been one of those rare occasions when they had nothing to do. They were embedded with marines outside Kandahar. Blake squatted in the shadow of an outcropping of rocks. The heat on the desert surface reached a boiling point.

She shielded her eyes against the blazing sun. "Yes. I know you love me," she assured him.

"Promise me, if anything happens to me, you'll get out of this. You'll leave the CIA."

She studied his expression, her smile fading. They'd had this discussion a few times in the past, but recently it seemed as if Blake brought it up more and more. It had become an obsession with him. Today, there was something in his eyes. He looked haunted almost.

"Nothing's going to happen to you, silly."

He wasn't smiling. She'd never seen him look so serious. His brown eyes searched her face as if memorizing every detail of it, and fear clawed at her heart. "I mean it, Erin. I don't want you to do this without me."

If he didn't sound so solemn, and if she wasn't feeling that icy cold slither of alarm, she might have been tempted to laugh. It was funny, considering Blake was the one who'd talked her out of leaving the CIA in the beginning, after she'd seen the darkest parts of their job. He'd told her she was a natural-born spy. She still wasn't sure if that was a compliment.

"I promise, okay, but nothing's going to happen, Blake. You're the best there is. What's got you so spooked? Is it this case?"

Blake had been working with his asset for more than a year now, putting the case together. Blake's contact, a man whose identity only Blake knew, was a Pakistani national with former Al Qaeda ties. They were in the final stages of bringing down the US's second most wanted terrorist in the world and breaking the back of one of the largest mobile insurgent training camps operating in and around the Afghanistan desert. If they were successful, this would be another major win for the War on Terror. Not quite as impressive as bringing Osama bin Laden down, but close.

Blake got to his feet and paced. "I don't know. I can't really explain it. It's just a feeling."

That in itself should have sent up all sorts of red flags. Blake didn't believe in feelings. He certainly wasn't the type of man to give into them.

Erin tried to think of something to ease his mind. "You're tired. This mission has been a long time coming. Once it's over, you should take some time off, go away somewhere."

He tried to smile, but it didn't quite reach his eyes. "Yeah. Maybe one of those tropical island paradises where they serve drinks with little umbrellas in them . . ."

Her eyes shot open. Cold sweat soaked her body. Erin stared at the ceiling, her breathing coming heavy. She could still see his smile, but it had been a dream. The reality of how senseless his death was warred with bittersweet memories the dream evoked. Closing her eyes tight, she tried to fall back to sleep. If she could have just a few more minutes with him. It didn't matter if it wasn't real.

Yet now when she closed her eyes images of that dreadful night taunted her instead, killing all the sweet memories and reminding her she would never share any of those special moments again with Blake.

Her body ached from the injuries. A severely sprained wrist, pieces of shrapnel embedded in her face, and three bruised ribs were a constant reminder of the night Blake died.

Getting out of bed was a struggle, as was dressing. Slowly Erin managed to pull on sweats and a T-shirt while ignoring the pain in her heart no amount of painkillers could take away.

The urn holding Blake's ashes still sat on the mantel of her fireplace, taunting her with the things she needed to do. Like bringing Blake's killers to justice. Getting out of this deadly shadow game before it claimed her life. Finding a final resting place for her big brother.

With the walls closing in and doubts swamping her like a tidal wave, she couldn't stay here any longer. Couldn't be alone. She grabbed her keys and headed out to be with the one person who shared her pain. Jax.

The streets of DC were slick, glistening in the streetlights. It had been raining for weeks, a fitting atmosphere for the gloom in her heart.

Erin pulled her car next to the curb near Jax's quiet home and killed the engine. Tomorrow was going to be a grueling day. Her first one back since Blake's death. She'd been dreading it for a while. With a final glimpse in the rearview mirror at the shadow of the woman she'd become, she forced her stiff limbs into action and climbed out of the car. Hitting the lock button, she stood outside Jax's house for a long time debating the wisdom of coming here. She needed to be close to someone who was close to Blake.

Ringing the doorbell, she half hoped he wouldn't be home. When the door opened, Jax stood before her dressed in jeans and a sweater, both accentuating his fit frame and sending her mind to places she wasn't ready to go. That he was still awake at this hour told her he had his own demons to wrestle with. There was no surprise in his blue eyes when he saw her standing on his stoop. He'd been expecting her. Of course, he would since she'd been here every night since she'd been released from the hospital.

Jax stood aside and let her pass through. The door closed. Seconds passed. Neither spoke. They were helping each other get through an impossible situation, she told herself, ignoring the fact that she'd come to lean on Jax way too much lately.

"Want some coffee?" he asked when she couldn't say anything.

She didn't, but she needed something to fill the time. "That'd be nice."

Erin followed him into the kitchen of his Washington, DC, brownstone. Watched as he poured two cups. Handed her one.

When the silence stretched out between them, she asked, "How's work? Anything new with the case?"

So far, even after digging for weeks, they'd come up empty-handed on identifying Blake's killers.

Jax shook his head. "Nothing. It's as if all our leads have dried up. The training camp in the desert disappeared. Our target, Al Hasan, is a ghost. There's been nothing from Blake's asset in weeks. I don't like it."

Erin didn't either. She couldn't help but believe something big was in the works. Without Blake's help, they might not be able to find out the truth until it was too late.

* * *

Every time Jax looked at her, his gut churned with guilt. He'd known going into the mission that something was off because of the way Blake was acting, and yet he hadn't tried to stop it.

Neutralizing the threat was imperative. In Jax's opinion, they needed more time to pull the mission together. But Blake had insisted. Al Hasan, the man they'd been hunting for months, was getting hinky, according to Blake's asset. Suspecting something was up.

Because he'd rejected his gut, Blake was dead and that truth had haunted him since he'd lost his friend.

Jax shoved the guilt aside. He'd dealt with it enough over the past month and it served no purpose. "Are you sure you're up to coming back to work tomorrow? It's only been a month," he said and regretted the reminder.

Erin set down her coffee cup and ambled toward the window. He could see all her doubts through the reflection in the window.

She sighed. "As up to it as I'll ever be." Pivoting, she faced him again. "I don't want to make a big deal of it. I just want to get it over with."

The emptiness in her eyes was hard to take. Erin had always been so alive before Blake's death. Full of energy, she was one of the best agents he'd had the pleasure of commanding. But death took its toll on them all.

Her raven hair hung down to her waist. Soulful green eyes seemed to look right through him. At almost six foot herself, Erin was a few inches short of his height, and they'd faced off many times over differing opinions.

"You should get some rest. You look tired. Want to crash here tonight?" he asked. His protective instincts ran deep where she was concerned. He wanted her close because he couldn't help but believe that the person responsible for Blake's death was closer than any of them thought, and Erin was an inadvertent eyewitness to what happened.

She shook her head, her answer not unexpected. "No, I'm fine. I . . . well, I needed to get out of the house for a second." She came close. His nerves hit the panic mode the same way they always did lately when she was near. He had no business feeling this way. She was his subordinate.

Erin stared at him with those haunted eyes and more than ever he wanted to take away her pain. He leaned close and touched his lips to hers. Just for a moment, yet feeling her lips against his was everything he'd dreamed of and her reaction exactly what he'd expected. With eyes wide, she swallowed visibly, stepped back, and made a beeline for the door.

Jax cringed at his own stupidity and followed after her, opening the door when she fumbled with it. He cleared the frog from his throat. "See how you feel tomorrow. If you're not up to it, then don't stress. You can come in the next day or the following week." He prayed his voice sounded steadier than he felt inside. He'd screwed up. Kissing her was the last thing he should have been doing.

Erin stepped out into the rainy night and turned to face him once more, her eyes capturing his. Residual doubts lingered in hers. "I want to be part of the investigation. I need to help bring Blake's killers to justice. I owe him that much."

He slowly nodded. "We all do." Their parting was awkward as usual. After a dozen different scenarios ran through his head, he finally leaned over and hugged her awkwardly. He felt her tense up briefly, then pull away, and his arms fell to his sides.

A ghost of a smile played on her lips. "See you tomorrow." She swiveled and headed to her car, but he couldn't move. His heart hammering, his feet planted in place, he watched her fire the car's engine and drive away without looking at him.

Foolish . . . he admonished himself. Why had he acted so unwisely? She needed his friendship. He wanted her love.

The DC night was warm for late fall, still a chill sped through his frame. He couldn't shake the feeling that something evil was imminent. With the uneasy feeling refusing to go away, Jax glanced down the street. His neighborhood was a quiet one. Most everyone had lived there for years.

Out of the corner of his eye, he noticed a dark SUV parked a short distance from his house. He didn't recognize it, and he knew all of his neighbors' vehicles.

Heading back inside, he killed the lights and crept to the window. The SUV hadn't moved. What was it doing there?

When the dread inside him continued to mount, he called it in.

"Hey, Jax, what are you doing up so late?" Dylan Gaines, one of the Special Activities Division team members assigned to him, asked. Jax could ask Dylan the same thing. It was closer to daybreak than it was night.

"I need you to run a vehicle description search for me." Jax gave him the information. He could hear Dylan typing.

"You know this is DC. There's a vehicle fitting that description stolen all the time. Why do you want me to run this one?" Dylan asked, no doubt curious by the odd request.

"Because it's parked near my neighbor's house, and it doesn't belong here."

"Got it . . ." The sound of keys being typed followed, then, "Wait, that's strange," Dylan said, and immediately Jax was on alert.

"What'd you find?"

"There is one vehicle fitting that description that was reported stolen last week, but get this. It belongs to the Afghan Embassy."

This grabbed Jax's attention immediately. Was it a fluke given that Blake had been killed in Afghanistan? The prickling at the back of his neck said differently.

"Strange coincidence, don't you think?"

Dylan took his time answering. "It is, but the vehicle was reported stolen."

Still, Jax couldn't let it go that easily. He crossed the room to the window once more. The SUV had vanished in the time it took him to place the call. "I'm sure you're right, but I want to talk to the person who drove the vehicle last, and I want to do it as soon as possible."

"All right." Dylan's audible sigh spoke volumes. Securing a meeting with anyone from the embassy at such a short notice would be difficult. "I'll see what I can set up for you tomorrow."

"Thank you, Dylan," Jax said and meant it. "I'm grateful for anything you can do. I'll see you in the morning." He ended the cal. With his Glock in hand, he went outside, slowly making his way over to where the vehicle had been parked. He panned the area. Was the parked SUV simply an accident or were they watching his place? Or Erin?

Jax dragged out his phone again and called her. "Hey, did you make it home okay?" he asked before she managed to say hello. Because he was now worried.

"Yes, I just got home." He could hear the questions in her tone. "Why?"

"No reason. I was worried about you, I guess." He regretted his choice of words. It hinted at more of a relationship than she was comfortable with, and he had just kissed her. Erin was a professional. She'd know the pitfalls of a romance between them.

"Okay." Her tone confirmed she didn't believe his excuse. After another awkward moment of silence, she said, "Well, I'll see you tomorrow." She ended the call in typical Erin fashion and

Jax went back inside.

Too restless to think about sleep, he dug out his dad's old Bible. Since losing Blake, he'd found himself returning to the faith of his childhood. The night of the funeral he'd scoured the Word of God and received comfort there. Since then, he'd found himself on his knees, begging for forgiveness and pleading for answers. But God, in His infinite wisdom, was being patient with His answers.

Chapter Two

Erin stared up at the place that was like a second home to her in the past. The Central Intelligence Agency in Langley, Virginia. The building promised protection. Freedom. Security. All a myth. It hadn't delivered any of those things for Blake. The job had taken away a good man.

As Erin stepped inside the entrance, she fought back the nausea at being here again. In the time since Blake's death, her grief had morphed to anger, then rage at the Agency that had yet to find his killers.

Today, within these once-hallowed halls, it was business as usual. For Erin, it wasn't the patriot business that brought her back. It was the need to get justice for Blake. If it were she who had died, Blake would go to the ends of the earth to find her killers.

"Erin, you're back!" Jennifer, the bleached-blonde receptionist spotted her immediately and hurried her way.

Erin forced a smile on her face. "Yes, I'm back."

Jennifer was the type of person who never met an enemy and wore her heart for the world to see. Compassion replaced her delight at seeing Erin again.

"I'm so sorry. I still can't believe he's gone." After a hug, Jen blinked back tears and linked her arm through Erin's. They walked toward the elevators together. For once, Erin was grateful for the company. She'd dreaded facing the rest of her unit again. They'd plied her with sympathy after the memorial service, but, as with most cases when someone close to you dies, people don't know what to say or do to make it better. She felt as if she'd lost part of herself.

More than seeing her colleagues again, she dreaded facing Jax. Lately, it seemed he was in her thoughts a little too much. He'd kissed her, forcing her to acknowledge there was more to her feelings for him then she wanted to admit.

He was her commander, her grief partner, Blake's best friend. And since Blake's death and their return to the States, he'd become the one she turned to for comfort.

As a closed-off ex-marine, Jax rarely spoke about his life outside the Agency. She'd once pestered Blake for information about his friend, convincing herself it was mild curiosity and nothing more. Now, she wasn't so sure. Something stirred inside her whenever she was with Jax. She stuffed those feelings down deep. She had a mission to perform. Nothing could get in the way of finding Blake's killers.

"Everyone's missed you so much. I'm glad your back. You should see the junk they pass off as coffee these days," Jen said.

Erin kept the smile glued on her face for Jen's sake. It was a running joke when she was away on a mission that the coffee around the Agency stunk to high heaven. Jen told her she was the only one who could brew a decent cup. "I'll have to see what I can do about that."

The elevator doors slid open, and, in a blink of the eye, she was back in the game again. She stepped out with Jen still close.

Breathe . . . she chanted in her head. *Just breathe. These people are your friends.*

It took only a few seconds before the people with whom she'd worked side by side through some of the worst possible times in history realized she was back. One by one, they came to her. Her comrades. The ones she was closest to gave her hugs. The rest extending their hands. Some couldn't quite make eye contact.

"How are you?" Sam Herring, one the best code-crackers around and a dear friend, waited until the crowd around her dwindled before asking.

Jen took this as her cue to return to her desk. She winked and said, "I'll catch up with you later. You want to have dinner at The Patriot this evening?"

Socializing—returning to normal—felt impossible. It hurt too much. Like a scab being ripped from the wound before its time. "Maybe. Check with me later." She felt as if the fake smile had been surgically stitched to her face.

Jen didn't take offense. "I understand. I'll grab you later for coffee."

Erin pivoted toward Sam. He was the type of guy who rarely smiled. Always so serious, he'd told her once that he'd been an introvert during school, spending most of the time in his room with his only friend, a computer.

"I'm taking each day and getting through it. So, I'm okay, I guess." She answered his previous question.

Sam nodded. "I miss him too. He was the only person I know who could beat me at War."

Erin swallowed back sorrow. It never ceased to amaze her how someone who lived the spy game in real time and had witnessed war firsthand could become almost addicted to a video game as Blake had. He and Sam had monthly gaming evenings where they played long into the night. Blake told her once it was because in the game he was in control. He could walk away from it whenever he wanted.

"I can still see him, clothes disheveled, eyes bloodshot, euphoric after one of your all-night gaming sessions."

"Yeah," Sam managed after clearing his throat.

"Have there been any breakthroughs on the . . . case?" She'd promised herself she wouldn't ask, yet she couldn't help it. She needed to know because she couldn't bear the thought of Blake's killers walking around free.

Sam appeared uncomfortable. "Not really," he said after a beat. "There's been nothing on the usual sites. No new chatter. It's almost as if they're waiting for our next move." Sam's gaze slid from her to focus on something behind her left shoulder, his brows raised.

"Erin, can I speak with you for a minute." Jax. His familiar, husky-sounding voice swept over her. She'd wondered how long it would take him to locate her.

Struggling to find the perfect blank expression, she faced him. Truth was, she didn't know how she felt about Jax Murphy most days. Since Blake's death, well, she owed him her sanity, yet she was pretty sure he wouldn't want her thanks.

Erin squeezed Sam's arm, then followed Jax into his office without a word. He closed the door softly, then waited while she made up her mind to sit.

"How are you holding up?" he asked, the calmness in his tone enveloping her.

She was sick of everyone asking her that ridiculous question, but managed to keep her disgust to herself. "I'm okay. I want to jump in and get busy. It's best that way."

His gaze slid over her face, and she felt the familiar rush of heat. Jax had the power to make her aware of him, even at the most inappropriate of moments. Like when she was barely keeping it together. Like now. She lifted her chin and waited for him to meet her eyes.

"Are you sure you're ready to be back at work?"

Her frazzled nerves couldn't let that statement go unchallenged. "You're back. He was your friend as well. Are you sure you're ready to be here?" Her tone was sharp, conveying her anger.

A muscle flexed in his jaw. She'd seen it many times in the past when their conversation turned adversarial. She'd gotten to him.

"But my friendship with Blake was different than yours. You were his partner. That relationship is closer than family most times. You trust your life to your partner. It's different," he stressed.

She lowered her eyes. After a second, she cleared her throat. "I'm fine. Really. I want to work."

Jax sat on the edge of his desk. "We need to talk about last night. Erin . . ."

Her pulse kicked out a crazy rhythm. He'd made a mistake by kissing her. She didn't want to hear his apologies. Waving her hand between them, she said, "No, we don't. You acted on an impulse and it's okay, I'm all right. We're all right. And frankly, I'm sick of talking. I've talked to the shrink. Friends. Acquaintances. Your pastor. Strangers. So, if it's all the same to you, we don't need to talk about what happened last night. All we need to do is find the people who did this to Blake before the trail goes cold."

He started to say something more, but thought better of it. "All right, we won't talk."

Erin rose to her feet, and, after a moment's hesitation, went into his arms. "It's okay. It will be okay, really. I know you're hurting, and that kiss last night didn't mean anything. It was blowing off emotions or whatever, so don't worry so much. We'll get through this." She looked into his eyes and saw confusion there.

He tensed briefly, nodded, held her tighter. She'd turned to him so many times since Blake's passing. In a weird way, spending time together had helped them both grieve.

Since Blake's death, she'd lost her edge. She needed to get it back if she was going to help find the people responsible for taking Blake's life. And she couldn't do that leaning on Jax.

She pulled away and avoided his eyes as she walked to the door, needing to put some space between them and the memories of the gentler side of Jax she'd seen last night. Their kiss was still fresh, drawing her in, confusing her, and making her feel again. She wasn't ready to feel.

"You must have left early this morning. I called, but you didn't answer." His words stopped her before she could escape. There was hesitation in his tone. He sounded uncertain. Impossible surely, from the man who'd held her as she'd cried at Blake's memorial service while never shedding a tear himself.

She forced herself to face him once more. His solemn expression made him look almost vulnerable. Exposed. "I went for a run, then showered and came here. I guess I missed your call." Had Blake's death cost him his edge as well?

He broke eye contact and nodded, the old Jax returning. Maybe it was her imagination.

"How can I help with the case?" she asked, making herself remain.

He moved behind his desk. "Erin, I know you want to be part of this, but you can't. You were too close to Blake. I'm not sure you can be objective."

Objective? Of course, she wasn't objective. "That's not fair and you know it. You and Blake were like brothers. I want to find his killers every bit as much as you do."

"I know you do, and we can use your help. I just can't let you go out in the field. It's too soon," he added when she would have protested the point. "I want you to go over the information we have leading up to that day. Everything we know so far. Finding Blake's asset is imperative. We missed something, Erin. The answers are there. Find them."

* * *

You must have left early this morning. I called, but you didn't answer.

He waited until the door closed behind her to let go of the breath he'd held inside, his whole body cringing at that foolish statement. Why had he told her that? He knew the score. Where they stood with each other. There could be no future for them. She'd needed him to help ease the pain. When she was strong again—and she would be soon—he'd go back to being her commander. Erin thought he shared the same wish. She had no idea it was different for him. If he was smart, she never would.

Every day, he missed Blake's quiet strength. His best friend was dead, killed while serving his country, and all Jax could think about was a woman whose only reason for associating with him beyond work was to make her pain bearable. He didn't much like the reasons, but he'd take her any way he could get her.

Staring into space, he realized he should be pushing to get his team on the ground in Afghanistan again. Working assets. Getting leads on Al Hasan, the man the CIA believed responsible for Blake's death, before the trail went ice cold, and it was well on its way there now. Instead, Erin was there in his head, a constant torment, and she was a subordinate at that. A romantic entanglement was the last thing he needed right now.

He sat at the desk he'd occupied since returning stateside and took the worn Bible from his backpack. Today, with his thoughts in turmoil, he desired the strength he'd always found in God's word now more than ever.

"I need Your peace," he whispered, then opened the Book to his favorite verses.

Let not your heart be troubled: ye believe in God, believe also in me.

In my Father's house are many mansions: if it were not so, I would have told you. I go to prepare a place for you.

And if I go and prepare a place for you, I will come again, and receive you unto myself; that where I am, there ye may be also.

He sat back and let the calming words wash over him.

A single knock sounded before his door opened. Dylan poked his head in. "I had to pull a whole lot of strings, but I got you a meeting at the Afghan Embassy with the ambassador's driver at one."

Jax blew out an impressed whistle. He knew how difficult the task was. "That couldn't have been easy. What's the man's name?" Jax dug through the desk drawer and found paper and pen.

"Ahmed Sediqi."

He did his best to spell the name correctly. "Great. I don't even want to know how you managed to pull that off, but thank you."

Dylan gave him a two-fingered salute before closing the door once more, and Jax stuffed the paper in his pocket.

He picked up the photo on his desk that was taken maybe a year earlier in Kandahar. It was his constant reminder, along with the emptiness he felt inside, of how much he'd lost—they'd all lost—to a war that so far couldn't be won.

The photo showed the six of them, as it was in so many cases. Kabir, then Jax standing next to Blake who was being his usual goofy self and making the peace sign above Erin's head. Well aware of her partner's antics, Erin was trying hard to keep a straight face. Dylan and Sam were in the background. They were all dressed in military fatigues. It was there, after a raid on a known terrorist hideout, that they'd found the crucial piece of evidence that would lead them to the safe house outside Belzadah, thanks to Blake's asset . . . and now the lead was responsible for Blake's death.

Since that dreadful day, Jax often wondered if perhaps Blake had some premonition about his future. He'd been . . . different.

A few days before they left on the mission, Blake had pulled him aside. Jax couldn't dismiss what he'd said that day. At first, Blake was so serious that Jax thought Blake might be about to ask him how long he'd been in love with Erin. He'd been expecting that question for a while.

They were hunkered down outside of Belzadah in the mountains. It was one of the longest nights of their lives. Until that final one.

"Jax, you need to pull Erin off this mission," Blake had said unexpectedly.

The statement wasn't anything close to what he'd expected. "Why?" he asked, startled by the request that was so unlike Blake.

Blake looked away, unable to maintain eye contact. Another out-of-character gesture. Blake was the most in-your-face type of guy Jax had ever met. "I don't know. I can't explain it. Call it a feeling, but just do it. You can order her off if you want. Tell her she's needed on another case. Tell her whatever you want, but don't let her go with me on this meet."

Baffled, Jax said, "I can't do that, and you know it. We need her. You know we barely have enough people to perform this mission as it is. I can't pull one of our best agents from a critical mission when we're so close to finishing. What's going on with you?"

Blake shook his head. "Nothing. I don't know. Like I said, I can't explain it. At least promise me if anything happens to me, you'll take care of Erin."

Jax couldn't make out Blake's expression in the moonless night. He'd tried to dismiss Blake's misgivings as pre-mission jitters. They all had them. "There's nothing going to happen to you. We've gone over the details. All the possible scenarios. We've got this."

Still, Blake didn't let it go. "I'm serious, Jax. I'm asking you as my friend. You're the only one I can trust. Make sure you look after her. Don't let anything bad happen to Erin, but don't let her know what you're doing. You know how hardheaded she is. She'll fight you every step of the way if she knows."

At a loss for what to say, Jax gave his word. He didn't like the direction the conversation had taken. It was bad luck to talk about such things the day before a mission. "You know I will, but nothing's going to happen to you. You've got a case of the jitters is all."

Blake whirled to face Jax. Fear in his eyes. A thousand times since that night, Jax wished he'd asked more questions. "Maybe. Still, I'm counting on you. And if something does happen to me, get her out of this mess. Get Erin out of the Agency. She deserves a life outside of all this."

He'd willingly agreed, and yet a month passed and he hadn't done a thing to fulfill his promises to Blake. He hadn't had a serious conversation with Erin since planning Blake's memorial service.

Truth was, he was having his own crisis because of work. He'd lost his drive. And worse still, he wasn't sure he believed in the cause anymore.

The phone on the desk buzzed, startling him out of the disturbing memory. He glanced at his watch, remembering the time. The debriefing. This one would be the hardest, because it was the first one Erin would be attending. She'd be forced to relive those gut-wrenching details, and they were no closer to bringing in Al Hasan than they had been that night.

Jax grabbed the receiver, said hello, and listened to Director Dean's assistant Phyllis as she informed him the director would like a word with Jax in his office before the debriefing.

"Did he say what this is about?" Jax asked, surprised by the request. It was foolish of him to try to glean intel from the director's assistant.

"No, but he's expecting you right away."

This wasn't good. Coleman Dean was a legend in the field in his day. He'd been part of the first wave of CIA agents to infiltrate Afghanistan when the War on Terror began following 9/11. Now, since he'd taken over as director, he was all about following procedure. He went through the proper channels to requisition a pencil. His orders always trickled down through the assistant director. An entourage of agents had surrounded Coleman at Blake's funeral. Which brought Jax back to his original assumption. Whatever Dean had to say wouldn't be good.

Jax took the elevator two floors up. The whole atmosphere on this floor exuded grandeur.

The director's personal assistant was waiting for him when he got off the elevator. "This way, Agent Murphy." She didn't wait for his answer as she spun, and he scrambled to keep up. Phyllis didn't stop until she stood in front of the double doors leading to the man whom some said held the future peace in Afghanistan, if not the entire Middle East, in his hands.

Phyllis opened the doors, stepped inside, and expected Jax to do the same. He followed her more slowly and waited while she closed the door once more. "Agent Murphy, sir."

Jax's attention locked on the man seated behind the opulent ash wooden desk. To say Coleman Dean could be intimidating was like saying summers were hot in Texas. The man wore his power like a very expensive suit.

Director Dean hadn't moved a muscle, and Jax wasn't sure what was expected of him. Before he could do anything, he realized the director wasn't alone. Peter Martin, the Assistant Director, and Jax's immediate superior, sat across from Dean. Another man stood at the window with his back to them.

"Thank you, Phyllis. That will be all," Director Dean commanded. Without a word, his assistant disappeared through the doors once more.

"Agent Murphy, have a seat." An order, not a request. While Jax walked the distance to the desk and sat, the man at the window turned toward them. It was the secretary of defense, Royce Kirkpatrick. Jax's previous misgivings kicked up another level.

Director Dean didn't bother with introductions. "You understand whatever is discussed within these walls stays within these walls. And I don't have to tell you what you are about to hear requires more than the utmost of confidentiality. It's a matter of national security."

Jax gave the director a nod in agreement then answered as an afterthought. "Yes sir, I understand."

Satisfied with Jax's answer, Director Dean nodded to the secretary of defense.

The gravity of the meeting was reflected in Kirkpatrick's stone-cold tone. "Agent Murphy, we have reason to believe the recent . . . happening in Afghanistan might not be the result of the enemy insurgents as first believed."

Jax tried to discern something from the SOD's expression, but the man seemed to have perfected the give-nothing-away stare.

"I'm afraid I'm not following you, sir."

Kirkpatrick glanced at the director before answering. "I'm saying someone on our side is responsible for what happened in Belzadah. Someone with very high clearance." He paused a moment as if to gauge Jax's reaction. "Someone from your team, Agent Murphy."

Someone from your team . . . It took a moment for the gravity of that accusation to sink in. Someone from his team a traitor? Impossible.

Jax bolted to his feet. His outrage wouldn't allow him to remain seated any longer. If he could have, he'd have walked out of the office and slammed the door. The one thing holding him back was the need to understand how the secretary of defense had come to such a drastic conclusion. There had to be some evidence to back his allegation.

Keeping his anger in check became a next-to-impossible feat. He gritted his teeth when he spoke. "With all due respect, Secretary Kirkpatrick, that's ridiculous. There's no way anyone from my team is a traitor. I vetted them myself personally. They are all patriots."

"Agent Murphy, you'd be well served to watch your tone," Director Dean barked out the rebuke, anger flushing his neck.

The SOD held up a hand. "It's okay, Coleman. I'm sure this is all coming as quite a shock."

"Jax, have a seat," his close friend Peter Martin urged under his breath.

Jax's first instinct was to leave the room and his superiors behind. Yet he sat back down because he needed to know the source of their suspicions. And that niggling in the back of his thoughts had him coming to the same conclusion. He endured the uncomfortable glances exchanged by the three men.

"I realize this has to be . . . difficult to hear, Agent Murphy. Learning that one of your comrades, and I dare say friends, might be working for our enemies abroad can't be easy, but I'm sorry to say there is no misunderstanding. Someone from your team is dirty. We aren't accusing anyone yet, but ferreting out the traitor is of utmost urgency. We can't afford to have one of our own betraying us." Kirkpatrick moved away from the window and took the remaining vacant seat. His sigh held the weight of the world on it.

"As you know, things have not gone as expected in Afghanistan. The loss of our troops and our agents is great. We can't afford any more disasters like the ambush in Belzadah, or the people of this country will demand someone be held accountable. The safe house in Belzadah was deemed secure less than twenty-four hours before that ambush. No one but your team knew about it. Which leads us to believe someone with intimate knowledge of the raid tipped off the insurgents that we were going to be there. It's imperative that we find the mole and bring that person to justice, if that hasn't already been accomplished."

If that hasn't already been accomplished?

It finally clicked what the secretary of defense was implying. "Wait, are you saying that you think Blake Robertson was the mole? That's preposterous. I knew the man well. He was my friend and one of the best agents the CIA ever produced. He wasn't the mole."

"Maybe not, but someone from your team is." Director Dean interjected with a hard edge to his tone.

Jax faced the director head on. "How do you know it isn't me? Or Peter, or even you, Director Dean?"

"Jax . . ." Peter's warning tone was easy to pick up on.

Jax knew he was treading on dangerous ground, yet he couldn't help it. What was being suggested was absurd.

The secretary of defense tried to smooth the waters. "It's okay, Peter. Agent Murphy has asked a legitimate question that needs to be addressed. The reason everyone in this room has been ruled out is because each of you has been handpicked by each other . . ."

"And my team was handpicked by me. I trust them with my life. You're looking in the wrong direction."

"You didn't let me finish," Kirkpatrick said. "Director Dean and Assistant Director Martin were in position long before these . . . incidents began to take place. You've been in the field since before Assistant Director Martin took over. The loyalty of the people in this room is not in question. So, with all due respect, Agent Murphy, someone from your team, Agent Robertson included, is a traitor, and we need your help to bring this person to light as quickly as possible."

"You want me to snitch on one of my own?" Jax asked in disbelief.

"That's not what he's saying at all. Don't you see that we have to figure out who did this? Lives are at stake. Our people are dying. We can't afford any more mistakes out there," Peter said.

Jax blew out a breath. He understood what Peter was saying, and he was right. The price in lives sacrificed for the war was already tremendous. If someone on his team was dirty, he wanted to know. If not, he wanted to clear their names.

"All right, I agree with you. What do you want me to do?" Jax had a feeling he wasn't going to like the answer.

The secretary of defense actually smiled. "Good. I appreciate what you have invested in your team, and I know this is hard. To start with, there will be a series of subterfuge missions taking place over the next few weeks. You'll give the orders, and you'll let one member of your team know the exact location we are targeting each time. Your team will perform the missions as if they were real. We'll need every member deployed. That means Agent Sandoval will return to active duty abroad immediately. Assistant Director Martin will be heading up today's briefing. He'll announce the first upcoming mission, keeping the details as brief as possible. As always, the location of the attack will not be disclosed to the rest of the team until they arrive."

Jax dismissed the idea of Erin going out in the field immediately. "Agent Sandoval isn't fit for active duty yet. It's too soon. She still has injuries, and she lost someone close to her. That takes its toll."

"We've all lost someone close to us." Director Dean made his disapproval crystal clear.

The secretary of defense arched a brow at the director before reining in the direction of the meeting to the point at hand. "I understand your concern—we all do—but in the interest of national security, I don't believe this can't wait."

"She'll be ready," Peter answered without sparing Jax a second glance. Jax would have argued, but his friend didn't give him the opportunity. "Secretary Kirkpatrick is right. This can't wait. Erin's a professional and a patriot. She'll do what she needs to do."

Jax got to his feet and headed for the door. "I hope you're right, Peter, because the battlefield is not the place to discover you're wrong."

Chapter Three

The moment Jax stepped into the debriefing room Erin could tell he had news about Blake's case. She scraped back her chair and got up. Before she reached his side, Assistant Director Peter Martin stepped into the room. Now was not the time. She returned to her chair and watched as Peter scanned the faces there until he spotted Jax's rigid frame leaning against one of the walls, arms crossed. Residual anger simmered between the two friends. She could see it from where she sat. Further emphasizing her belief that something big had happened.

Peter moved to the head of the room. "Good morning, everyone. Let's get started," Peter said. "We have a lot to cover. First, I appreciate how hard everyone's working to find Blake's killers, so I'll be brief."

Peter was taking the lead when normally briefings were all Jax's. Something was clearly off.

"There's important news. Blake's contact reached out to me recently. He wants to keep working with us," Peter announced, the information snapping Erin's head toward the front of the room. She recalled something Blake had said once about the asset. He told her the man trusted no one. He'd refused to speak with anyone but Blake. What changed his mind?

"Our asset has given us what we believe to be the current location of Al Hasan, the man behind the attack at Belzadah according to the asset. I don't need to tell any of you that we have to act quickly on this."

Peter brought up drone photos showing a desert area some distance from Kabul. The location appeared close to the Mendiu Pass, a porous gateway into Pakistan and a known Al Qaeda passageway.

The photos showed an unusual amount of activity around a village, but there was no sign of the training camp that had previously been their target.

"This was the last known location of the camp. It has since moved, but our asset assures me it is close, as is Al Hasan."

Erin studied her teammates' reactions. Dylan Gaines and Sam Herring had both been part of the team since its inception. Their doubt was evident in their expressions. Tyler Barrett, another agent, had joined the debriefing. No doubt he'd be taking Blake's place.

"You leave for Afghanistan tomorrow at 0200 hours. As you know, the journey will be difficult. You'll be heading into some dangerous territory where enemies of the US are everywhere. Taliban, Al Qaeda, unfriendly tribesmen, not to mention a few desert creatures that could be as lethal as any carefully placed bomb. Most locals have no idea about the friendly agreement between the US and the Afghan nation." Peter glanced around at the people seated there.

"I suggest you all get some rest. It's going to be a rough couple of days. Since the team is a man short, we'll be adding Tyler Barrett to this mission. Tyler, get with Jax. He'll bring you up to speed on what you need to know. More details will be made available once the team is in the country, and as needed. In light of what happened to Blake, details will be made available on a need-to-know basis only. I'm sure you can appreciate the necessity of confidentiality. Lives are at stake here, people. We can't afford another death."

Peter paused for a second. "Questions?" he asked the shocked room. No one spoke up. "Good. Then, I'll see you all tomorrow morning." Without another word, Peter left the room.

After the initial shock wore off, voices jumbled together asking questions. "How does Peter know this is the same guy that Blake trusted?" Dylan asked with skepticism before he turned to Erin. "Did Blake ever mention the asset's name to you?"

She shook her head. "No, never. As far as I know, the man trusted no one but Blake." She looked to Jax. "What if this guy isn't Blake's contact at all? We could be walking into another setup."

Jax held up his hands. "It's legit and that's all I can say. You heard Peter. We're a go. I suggest you prepare for this assignment because it's going to be a difficult one." Without looking at her, Jax left the room, leaving stunned silence in his wake.

"Well, I, for one, don't like it." Sam was the first to speak. "Something feels off about this." Several of the others nodded, Erin among them. But what choice did they have? If there was even the slightest chance this man was Blake's contact, and they could capture Al Hasan and bring him to justice for taking Blake's life and the lives of others, they had to take it.

Promise me, if anything happens to me, you'll get out of this. You'll leave the CIA. I don't want you to do this without me. Reality dawned hard. She was going back into the field. Could she handle it without Blake?

Erin glanced around the room and realized it was empty. An uneasy chill sped down her spine. This new mission—being back here without Blake—sent her emotions into turmoil.

She rose to her feet and headed past Jax's office. She wanted to get out of here as quickly as possible.

The door stood open. Jax spotted her.

"Erin, hang on a second," he said.

The last thing she wanted was another emotional conversation with him. She struggled to recapture her composure. Thinking of Blake brought back so many painful feelings. At times, she could almost see him smiling. Hear his laughter.

Jax stood in the doorway of his office watching her. A moment later, he retreated inside, and she reluctantly followed. He held something in his hand. She realized it was a photo she knew by heart.

He saw her looking at the photo and shook his head before placing it back on his desk. "Are you sure you're up to going back there?" he asked, not unexpectedly. He was worried about her. He'd seen how emotionally shattered she'd been. Still was.

All she could do was be honest with him. "I have no idea, but I want to be part of it. If we have the chance to bring Al Hasan down, I'm not missing out."

His gaze dropped to the desk. He didn't like her answer. "It won't be easy. We're heading into some bad country."

Erin knew all his concerns by heart because she shared them. "Don't worry. I can carry my weight."

His face twisted as if in pain. "I'm not concerned about that. You're one of the best agents I've ever worked with, but you've been through a lot lately. I'm worried about *you*."

Erin clasped his hand. "Don't be. I'm okay." He glanced down at their entwined fingers, a muscle working in his jaw. At once, feelings that had no place happening between them resurfaced. She remembered the gentleness of his kiss the night before. Her own awakening to it.

"I have to go," she said and pulled her hand free. "I have some errands to run before the trip." She stumbled over the words, blindly heading for the door.

He followed her. "Erin . . ." Her name came out in a ragged whisper. She reached for the door handle. Before she could turn it and escape, he covered her hand with his. What was wrong with her? This was Jax, her commander. Her friend.

Jax gently turned her to face him. "I'm sorry I stepped out of line yesterday. I shouldn't have kissed you." The words threatened to cut the knees out from under her, and she struggled to hold onto her composure.

"It's okay." She managed what passed for a smile. "We've been through a lot together. There's bound to be some residual feelings." It was a lame excuse and one he didn't like.

"I guess you're right." His hands dropped and he stepped back, his gaze cold. "You should get some rest. Tomorrow will be difficult." He turned away, the change in him like a knife to her heart.

Erin clenched her hands tight. She could feel the prickle of tears so close. Facing the door again, she didn't want him to notice.

"I'm sorry," he murmured so low that she almost didn't hear.

"For what?" She struggled and somehow captured her blank expression before turning to him once more.

"For springing this on you. For sending you back into the field so soon. I just found out before the briefing. I wish . . ."

It was there again. That look on his face she couldn't define. It had her curious. "What? What do you wish?" She couldn't explain it, but she wanted to understand him. What he felt. The secrets he kept inside.

He looked so lost that she touched his face, surprising them both. He captured her hand in his and kissed her palm sending shivers speeding down her spine.

Jax shook his head. "Nothing. I just wish that you didn't have to go back there."

Don't let it get too intimate, her heart urged. Using all her willpower, she stepped back, and he let her go. "I'll be fine. I want to . . . help." Her voice faltered over the word. She wanted to make the person responsible for taking Blake's life pay dearly.

Jax's brows knitted together. He hadn't missed her slip. "Are you sure that's all you want?" he asked quietly.

She took another step backwards, so she could breathe again. "What do you mean?" But she knew.

"Killing Al Hasan or a thousand other terrorists like him won't bring Blake back."

She blew out a breath and broke eye contact. "I know that," she mumbled without looking at him.

Jax stepped closer and she steeled herself. She wouldn't back away.

"Erin, Blake . . ." He stopped. His expression pained.

"What about Blake?"

Jax shook his head. "Blake wanted you to get out of this life. He didn't want you to keep doing this."

What he had to say was too close to her dream. Erin spun on her heel, tossing her words over her shoulder. "Yeah, well, Blake's dead. I'm not. I have to keep going. I have to live."

And right now, to do those things, she needed to get away. From this place. Jax. These people. They were a constant reminder of Blake, and it was like living the loss all over again.

Erin hurried out of his office and past Jen, who, thankfully, was on the phone and distracted. She barely made it to her car before the panic took hold. She struggled to open the door and climb inside the sanctuary of her vehicle. She scanned the parking area as if expecting Al Hasan to emerge from the shadows.

With the silence of the car settling around her, she breathed out, let what was bottled up inside of her come out, and then she screamed and slammed her fist against the steering wheel until there was nothing left inside her but emptiness.

* * *

Jax arrived at the Afghan Embassy shortly before the appointed time, where he'd been asked to wait in the lobby for almost an hour—the request cordial but guarded. Finally, he was ushered into an office to meet with the driver.

"Thank you for meeting with me, Mr. Sediqi." Jax addressed the solemn-faced man.

"It is no problem. Ambassador Nuristani asked me to give you my full cooperation. I am at your service. How may I help you, Agent Murphy?"

"You reported the Embassy's SUV missing two weeks ago, is that correct?" While Jax held a pad and pen in his hand, he kept his focus on the man's facial expression. Nothing changed. Either Sediqi had perfected the deadpan stare or he was hiding something.

"Yes, that is correct. I'd finished cleaning it earlier in the day, and I parked it in front of the embassy in preparation for the ambassador's evening out at the opera. He normally attends every Thursday. He and his wife have dinner out first. One hour later, when I went to start the vehicle, it was gone. I reported it missing to the local police. They came and took the report, but were not very reassuring about its recovery, though. So far, they were right to have doubts. The vehicle has not yet turned up."

Sediqi's story was a little too convenient for Jax's tastes. Why would the man leave the embassy's vehicle parked out front when there was secured parking beyond the gates and the crime rate for stolen cars in DC continued to rise each year?

"I'd like to see the security footage from the camera in front of the embassy, if I may. Perhaps I can discern the perp's ID from it and help you recover the missing vehicle."

Sediqi blinked several times and appeared to grow uncomfortable. "I'm afraid that would be impossible. As it turns out, the camera was not working properly. When the vehicle first went missing, the embassy's security team reviewed the camera feed. Sadly, nothing recorded."

Not for a minute did Jax believe him. What he didn't understand was why the driver was being so evasive.

"Still, I'd like to check it for myself," Jax insisted.

Sediqi broke eye contact. "You would need to speak to Ambassador Nuristani about that. I have no control over the workings of the security team."

Jax hid his frustration badly. If the vehicle was stolen, wouldn't the embassy want to do everything in its power to recover it?

His thoughts went to the SUV watching his place. He hadn't noticed it before, but then again, he hadn't been looking. Was it the first time it had been parked outside? He thought about asking his neighbors, but didn't want to alert them to trouble unnecessarily.

"You can be sure I will do that." Jax assured the man. A flash of anger took life in Sediqi's eyes. Had he been expecting Jax to let the matter go?

Sediqi bowed his head. "Very well. If there is nothing more?"

Jax blew out an annoyed-sounding sigh and slowly nodded. Sediqi excused himself and hurried away while Jax watched him disappear through the same double doors he'd walked through a short time before.

Rubbing a hand across his neck, the story was becoming more and more tangled. He returned to the receptionist's desk. The young woman seated there met his gaze with an unwavering look.

"I'd like a word with Ambassador Nuristani, please."

With raised brows, the young woman took her time answering. "I'm sorry, the ambassador has a very busy afternoon. May I ask what this is regarding?"

Jax held onto his patience with difficulty. "It's about the embassy's stolen vehicle. I'd like to check the feed from the security camera out front." He waited while the young woman wrote the note.

"I will pass the request along to the ambassador's assistant. Perhaps he will have a moment to spare. Excuse me, please." She stepped through the double doors behind her. A second woman focused her full attention on the computer screen in front of her, ignoring Jax entirely.

He stepped back from the counter and milled around, ending up at the windows facing out to the street. The camera in question was positioned to catch every movement in front of the embassy for a reason. Security for foreign dignitaries was always of grave importance. The camera would have been checked periodically to insure it was in working order. He didn't believe that it hadn't captured any images. Whatever was on the tape, the embassy didn't want it to be made known to him or the local PD for a reason. Did it show someone from the embassy taking the vehicle? Perhaps Sediqi?

A noise behind him, someone clearing a throat, sent Jax whirling at the sound. The woman had returned, her face giving away nothing.

Jax approached the desk.

"I'm afraid the ambassador is unavailable. I'll have his assistant call you when he has some time."

Her message was loud and clear. There would be no further help coming from the embassy or the ambassador.

"Thank you for your time," Jax told the young woman and then turned and left the building, stepping out into a relatively clear afternoon.

Afghanistan was a US-friendly country, and yet he'd gotten nothing but shutdown from the moment he entered the embassy. Sediqi was hiding something. Had the vehicle been stolen at all? What if Sediqi was following Jax for some reason?

An uneasy feeling slithered into the pit of his stomach. He couldn't dismiss the notion that his treatment today and the vehicle parked close to his place were connected to Blake's death in some way.

Jax unlocked his car and climbed behind the wheel, tapping a rhythm with his fingers while reviewing his options. Ahmed Sediqi told him that he'd reported the missing vehicle to the DC police. He'd call his buddy in major crimes and see what he could find out.

After squeezing into the heavy traffic in front of the embassy, Jax dialed his friend's number and waited.

"Detective Alexander," Lane answered in a hurried tone. Jax couldn't imagine Lane's caseload. The DC police were overworked as the crime rate continued to soar in the capital city.

"Lane, it's Jax. Got a minute?"

In the background, Jax heard a door close. "For you? Of course, I do. What's up?" He and Lane had grown up together outside of DC, both attending the University of Virginia. After university, they'd taken different career paths.

Jax explained about the stolen SUV.

"Let me take a look into the police report, and I'll call you back later today when I know more."

"Thanks, Lane, I appreciate it. How's Molly?" Jax had been best man at Lane and Molly's wedding. They'd kept in touch through the years, but Jax hadn't gotten together with his friend in a long time.

"She's doing well. Our first child is due in two months."

Jax still couldn't imagine Lane being a father. As kids, they'd gotten into trouble more times than not. It was ironic that Lane had gone into law enforcement, and Jax was in the CIA.

"I can't wait to see you as a dad," Jax laughed. "After all the stuff we pulled as kids, payback is going to be rough."

Lane joined in the humor. "What about you? When are you going to settle down? Give up the spy business for good."

The question was an uncomfortable one. If Lane had asked it a year ago, he'd have answered never, but his growing feelings for Erin had shaken him to the core. With Erin, he could imagine settling down. Giving up the shadow games. "Not anytime soon, unfortunately, since business is booming, but I can't wait to spoil your child, then give him back to you."

Lane chuckled. "Sounds like something you'd do. Anyway, I'll give you a call back when I have information."

For once, Jax was happy to let his friend go. Erin was a touchy subject and one he didn't want to get into with Lane. Every time he was near her, he went up in flames. He wanted more. Wanted her heart. Wanted the impossible.

Once the call ended, he crawled along with the heavy traffic. He felt pulled in a dozen different directions. The earlier meeting with the secretary of defense and Director Dean had him on edge. He couldn't let himself believe someone from his team would betray their country in such a way, it didn't matter what the higher-ups claimed to have. Why had the SOD mentioned Blake in particular? It was bad enough that he'd died trying to protect his country, now his good name was being dragged through the mud.

Jax clicked off each member of the team in his head, including their newest, Tyler. He'd evaluated them all personally. Knew about their pasts. Their likes. Dislikes. Their families. They were all good people. Whatever evidence Kirkpatrick thought he had, he was looking in the wrong direction.

In spite of his misgivings, the briefing had gone smoothly enough. No one on the team had a clue that the mission they were scheduled to leave on tomorrow morning was a ruse. He'd take Sam aside and tell him the exact location of the meet, then see what happened. He prayed this wasn't going to prove to be a waste of valuable time they could use to hunt down Al Hasan.

The entire team believed they would be pursuing a lead from Blake's asset. He hated lying to the people who had his and each other's backs, but he had no choice. He was following orders, but more than anything, he wanted to prove the allegations being lodged against his team wrong.

Jax pulled into the drive of his home. Today, no strange vehicles were parked down the street. Nothing out of the ordinary. Had he been wrong about the vehicle belonging to the embassy? Dylan was right. Dozens of vehicles were stolen around DC on a weekly basis. Many resembling the SUV he'd seen. Why couldn't he let it go? There was enough to worry about with the upcoming fake mission.

He barely made it through the door when his cell phone rang. Jax dropped his backpack that held his laptop onto the floor by the door and dug the phone out of his jeans pocket. Lane's number popped up on the screen.

"You have news for me?" Jax asked without a hello.

"I do. You were right about a report being filed on the missing SUV, but we ran into the same results as you did. Our detectives were told the camera outside the embassy was on the fritz. So, basically, I have nothing new for you. For what it's worth, the lead detective working the case didn't buy the story about the camera being broken either. He checked it out. Said the camera was working fine. No reason why it shouldn't have captured the perp."

Jax glanced out the window at the quiet street in front of his house. "What are they hiding?" Whatever it was, it had to be important.

"I don't know," Lane said with an audible sigh. "But I'm guessing it has to do with more than a missing vehicle."

The thought was a disturbing one because it matched his own. "You're right. It does." Jax ended the call and tried to deny the unease in the pit of his stomach. He couldn't get it out of his head that there was more going on with the missing embassy SUV than what those surrounding it were willing to divulge, and he was positive it connected to Blake's death somehow.

Shoving aside his unease, Jax grabbed the backpack. Carrying it to the bedroom, he began packing for the upcoming mission while resisting the urge to call Erin and tell her everything. He'd lost his anchor. In the past, he'd been able to talk to Blake about things that troubled him. Now, he felt as if he were on an island with dangerous waters churning all around.

With no one to talk to, he called Peter, even though he was still angry with him.

"I'm glad you called," Peter said quietly, as if reading his thoughts. "I'm sorry about the way things went today. I know you felt blindsided by the news, but I was asked not to say anything."

Jax stuffed down his anger. Peter was only doing his job. "I know you couldn't mention it, but you of all people know Blake would never do what Kirkpatrick suggested. None of the team would, for that matter."

The length of time it took for Peter to answer assured Jax his friend didn't agree. "I know this is hard, but I'm afraid it's not only possible but likely."

Peter wouldn't be so convinced if he didn't have solid proof. "What do you know?" Jax asked, tone sharp, knowing his friend wouldn't be able to answer that question.

"I can't say, but the evidence is reliable. Someone on the team is definitely dirty, and we have to find out who the mole is and fast before someone else dies."

If he'd been looking for comfort, Peter's words fell woefully short.

"I'll see you all before you head out in the morning," Peter said after the silence stretched out between them. Jax ended the call without responding.

It was still the middle of the day, and Jax was too restless to sleep. He couldn't get the strange reaction he'd received at the embassy out of his head. On an impulse, he called Dylan, knowing he'd be at the office. Dylan was a workaholic who did his best work on little sleep.

"You know you should be getting some rest," Jax told him. "We've got a tough road ahead of us."

"As should you," Dylan shot back, without concern that Jax was his superior. "What's up?"

Jax wasn't sure how to approach the subject, so he took the straightforward approach. "How good are you at hacking?" The uncomfortable silence that followed his question confirmed how odd the request was.

"Good. Why do you want to know?" Dylan asked, clearly surprised by the question.

Jax knew he was asking Dylan to go against the law, but he needed answers. "Can you see if you can get me the recordings for the camera outside the Afghan embassy? I'm sure they have it stored somewhere on their system." He told Dylan about his meeting with the driver and the dismissive shoulder he'd received from the ambassador. "They're hiding something. I want to know what."

Chapter Four

She hated this place. Hated what it represented. The CIA Memorial Wall was one of the first things visitors saw when they entered the Original Headquarters Building in Langley. The wall—located on the north side, stood as a silent memorial to those CIA employees who died in the line of duty. The Honor and Merit Awards Board had received the recommendation from Coleman to add Blake's star to the wall. The board expedited the request, and the ceremony took place as a memorial service a few weeks after the team returned from Afghanistan.

Erin traced her finger over the last two-and-one-half-inch star on the row. Blake's.

She searched the Book of Honor, sandwiched between the US flag and the one bearing the CIA emblem, for Blake's name.

In honor of those members of the Central Intelligence Agency who gave their lives in the service of their country.

She'd read those words a dozen times. It wasn't just their lives that were sacrificed on the country's altar; it was the wives, friends, parents, and children there with them. She'd heard the word used to define Blake. Patriot. Now, her hands shook. She was furious. Had been since the day the truth finally sank in and she realized her best friend wasn't ever coming home. She still didn't understand why. But, today, like all the other times, these hallowed halls kept their secrets. No answers echoed from the names listed here.

She touched the cross given to her by her parents. Growing up, she went to church every time the doors were open, her faith strongly secure in God's grace. But, lately, that faith had taken a beating. Anger and bitterness controlled her heart. She was furious with everyone, including God, and she hated being this way. Blake wouldn't want that for her.

Controlling the tears was hard, but she laid her heart bare before God.

I need You now. I don't know why this happened, and I'm just so angry and embittered. Please, help me. Erin slowly opened her eyes. Her only answer was the gentle sound of the AC system above, taking the Indian summer heat away. Still, a calmness she hadn't felt in a long time enveloped her like a warm blanket.

She touched Blake's star once more. "I'll always love you, brother. And I promise I'll learn the truth behind your death, and then I'll find a good place for you to rest." Wiping tears away, she pivoted and left the building. Shielding her eyes against the late afternoon sun, she headed to her car. She needed to go home. Prepare for what was ahead. Going to Afghanistan would be impossible under most conditions, but being there now after losing Blake, well, it was going to be an emotional experience, and she wasn't sure how much more emotion she could handle.

Starting the car's engine, Erin pulled out onto the street. A vehicle was parked on the opposite curb. A blacked-out Suburban. As she drew closer, something about the SUV grabbed her attention and anxiousness pooled in her stomach. Heading toward the vehicle, she could see at least two heads inside. As she passed the vehicle, she noticed no license plate on the front. Glancing in her rearview mirror proved there wasn't one on back either. A shiver ran down her spine. Something about the vehicle sent up alarms.

She kept her speed steady as she continued down the road. Another look in the rearview mirror and she spotted the Suburban making a U-turn. Fear made it hard to breathe. She couldn't lead them to her house.

Even after several evasive moves, the SUV remained several car lengths behind her.

Erin pulled into a fast food drive-through and saw the vehicle slow briefly, then speed past. This was no accident. Those men were following her.

She ordered burgers and fries, then paid and pulled back around to the front, making sure the vehicle was nowhere in sight. Erin needed to tell someone, and there was only one person she trusted.

Still uncertain about the vehicle's location, she waited an additional half hour before leaving the parking lot. With her body on full alert, Erin drove through the familiar neighborhood and parked in front of Jax's house. His car was out front instead of in the garage as if he'd been in a rush to get inside.

Shoving aside the myriad of emotions that swamped her heart, Erin grabbed the bag of burgers and got out. She panned the area. The SUV was nowhere in sight. Without hesitating, she dashed to the door.

Jax answered before she hit the doorbell. Had he been watching? What had him feeling so uneasy? She held up the bag. He slowly smiled, opened the door wide to let her in, then stepped outside and gave a quick look around.

Something troubled Jax, and she was spooked enough to believe it might be related to her tail from earlier. "What's going on?" she asked, dropping the burgers on the coffee table, her brows slanted upward. Fear caused goosebumps to form on her arms.

Jax shut the door and faced her without making eye contact. "I don't know what you mean."

"You were checking for something. You answered the door before I even rang the bell. What is it, Jax?"

The worry in his blue eyes was undeniable. After several seconds ticked by without him answering, he blew out a breath and said, "Nothing really. I'm on edge, I guess. It's this upcoming mission. I guess after what happened to Blake, well . . ." He left the rest unspoken, but he wasn't telling the whole truth. "Those burgers smell delicious. Let's dig in."

Erin forced her misgivings aside for the moment. As her commander there were things Jax couldn't tell her, but still . . .

He grabbed a couple of sodas from the fridge and handed her one while she took the burgers and fries from the bag and put them on plates, warmed them in the microwave, and then carried them back to the coffee table.

Jax dug into his burger while she snuck covert glances his way. Even the way he sat accentuated his edginess. She would have liked to help ease his mind, but he'd chosen not to tell her what was really troubling him. It seemed to drive home the truth of their relationship. Jax was her commander. Nothing more.

That reality cut like a knife. In time, perhaps, her feelings for him would fade. He'd been there for her when she needed a shoulder to lean on. She was grateful for his gentle hugs. The times he'd let her cry without saying a word. She'd seen that tender side of him that few people knew. Jax Murphy was a kind and caring person.

"As nice as this is, you know you should be home resting," he said once he'd finished his burger, wiping his hands on a napkin. "Tomorrow is going to be a grueling day, and you're still not a hundred percent."

She dismissed his concern with a wave of her hand. "I'll be fine. I could do this in my sleep." Should she tell him about the vehicle that followed her?

He grabbed his soda and took a sip, his piercing eyes taking in every detail on her face. "Is something wrong?" he asked, correctly interpreting her worries.

She hesitated. "I'm not sure. I stopped by the Wall of Honor earlier." He would understand her need to be close to something related to Blake. He'd told her he'd done the same thing many times. "But when I left the building, a vehicle was parked across the street from me. An SUV." What if she'd been wrong? The driver could have just been traveling the same way as she was. She was a trained agent, not someone who jumped at her shadow. Her gut confirmed she wasn't mistaken about the vehicle's intention.

"Jax, I know this sounds crazy, but I'm almost positive they were following me."

That she had his full attention was clear. "What type of SUV?" The muscle working in his jaw told her he was taking what she said seriously and it didn't come as a surprise to him.

Her brows knitted together in a frown. Something else was going on. "I don't know. I think a Suburban. It was definitely black."

Jax jumped to his feet and strode to the window, looking out as if expecting someone to be waiting there. She followed him and peered outdoors.

"What are you looking for?" she asked, scanning the quiet street. Nothing unusual appeared.

"Your Suburban." He faced her, mere inches separating them. Her heart was doing its usual somersault at his nearness.

Erin swallowed deeply. "What do you mean, my Suburban?"

What Jax had to say was frightening. The vehicle had been parked outside his home the night before. Her instincts were right. The vehicle's appearance wasn't an accident.

"It has to be the same SUV, but why is it following us?" She couldn't make sense of it. Couldn't dismiss the premonition that it was related to Blake's death.

He shook his head. "I don't think they're following us. I'd say they're following you. The vehicle was here when you left the other night, but not for long. They're tailing you, Erin, and I have no idea why."

The nervousness pooling in her limbs told her she wasn't going to like the answer to that question when it came. "You think this has something to do with Blake?"

He met her gaze, the truth clear in his eyes before he spoke. "I think it's a good possibility." He stopped for a moment, then said, "Stay here tonight. I have plenty of room. We can go to your place in the morning to get your things before heading out to Langley."

Though the offer sounded tempting and the prospect of returning to an empty house terrifying, she shook her head and headed for the door. "No, I should go."

He followed her. As she turned to face him before leaving, she could see all the worries on his drawn face. She reached up and touched his cheek briefly before opening the door. "Don't worry so much. I'll be okay. I do know what I'm doing." She faked a smile that he didn't return.

"Be careful," he told her instead. "We aren't sure what we're up against, and I don't want anything to happen to you."

With those chilling words standing between them, she headed to her car. Spooked, her eyes darted around the quiet neighborhood, her heart thundering.

As much as she wanted to take him up on his offer, the other danger—just as frightening as someone following her—was being close to Jax all evening.

* * *

Jax had never felt so frustrated. Dylan called shortly after Erin left. He'd hacked into the embassy's security system. The camera feed had been deliberately wiped clean.

Danger lurked all around. Closing in. Suffocating them. Yet every time he was near Erin, all he could think about was how he felt about her. The way she kept him at arm's length assured him his feelings weren't reciprocated.

This whole lie he'd been ordered to tell the team went against everything Jax believed in. He hated lying to his people. Hated that the higher-ups believed someone from his unit was dirty. It went beyond his ability to accept—yet Peter had all but confirmed that they had the evidence to back up the claim.

With nothing but the rest of the day stretching out in front of him and his misgivings growing, Jax knew he had to get out of the house if he stood a chance at keeping it together.

He grabbed his keys and headed outdoors. Driving through the light afternoon traffic toward the downtown area, only one place came to mind.

Outside Blake's old apartment building, he stared up at the ten-plus floors. He'd been here dozens of times in the past. He and Blake used to hang out, watching a game on TV or discussing their latest mission. So many good times were memorialized inside the four walls of Blake's apartment.

Jax slowly climbed out of the car. Since Blake's death, he refused to set foot in the place. He knew it was past time to clean the place out, even though according to Blake's landlord the rent was paid up for another couple of months. His friend had no living relatives. Erin, Jax—the team was his family.

He took out the key Blake had given him, unlocked the door, and went inside. The stillness froze him in place, reminding him of the finality of death. The person who'd lived here wasn't coming back. The cares of this world were over for Blake.

All around, the last moments of Blake's life stateside unfolded before him. In the kitchen, he'd left a box of cereal sitting on the counter. The closet door was open in the bedroom. A piece of clothing hung from one of the dresser drawers, as if Blake had packed in a hurry. The unmade bed just about reduced Jax to tears.

Why had he come here? What was he expecting to find?

It's imperative that we find the mole and bring him to justice, if that hasn't already been accomplished. He couldn't get Kirkpatrick's accusations out of his head. It cast doubts on all the good work Blake had done. He loved his country. He deserved better than to have the blame laid at his feet postmortem.

Jax began opening drawers in the kitchen, not sure what he was looking for. The usual array of utensils and junk filled most of the drawers, along with way too many take-out menus. Blake hated to cook. Jax could count on one hand the times he'd seen his friend prepare a meal.

When the kitchen gave up nothing useful, Jax continued his search in the living room. What was he expecting to find? Perhaps something to prove Blake's innocence once and for all.

In the desk shoved in the corner of the living room, he found a receipt to a safety deposit box. Jax did a double take. As far as he knew, Blake never mentioned having one. What was in it? Uneasiness crawled up his spine. Jax glanced at his watch. Even though Jax had Blake's power of attorney, it was too late to check on the box today. As soon as he returned from Afghanistan, he'd investigate. See what Blake felt the need to protect.

Beyond the receipt, he located a bank statement for a branch bank. Blake had a small savings account and little money in his checking.

Jax blew out a breath, letting go of his momentary doubts. If Blake were taking bribes to betray his country, it sure wasn't reflected in his bank statement. He shook his head. It was just this assignment. The accusations that were lodged. While there had to be enough evidence for Kirkpatrick and the director to act on, Jax was positive they were wrong about his team, and he intended to prove it.

He gave the apartment one final glance, then left. When this thing blew over, he'd get with Erin. Together they'd go through Blake's possessions and clear out the apartment.

Back outside, the rain had begun again, chilling the early evening air. Jax slid into his car and eased out into the thickening traffic, trying to prepare himself for what must be done.

A glance in the rearview mirror had him sitting up straighter. Parked a hundred yards away was the same SUV that he'd seen outside his home. Probably the same one who'd followed Erin.

Jax braked, the car behind him almost slamming into him, before he did a U-turn in the middle of the road. The car behind honked his annoyance. Several other drivers joined in. He knew he was drawing attention to himself, but Jax was determined not to let the driver of the SUV get away this time.

He drove back to the location where it was parked. The vehicle hadn't moved. Jax whipped into the closest parking space and sprang out of the car. With weapon drawn, he hurried toward the Suburban. "Get out of the vehicle with your hands up."

His order was met without a response. Jax was aware of calling unwelcome attention to himself from several people passing by. When you brandished a weapon in public, you drew attention. It wouldn't be long before the DC police arrived.

Advancing on the driver's side door, Jax looked inside. The vehicle was empty. He quickly shoved his weapon behind his back and out of sight.

Being as careful as he could, he took the edge of his jacket and opened the driver's door, peering inside. The vehicle looked as if it had been wiped clean. He could smell the chemicals.

Jax grabbed his phone and called it in to Lane. "I have your stolen vehicle." He gave Lane the location.

"How'd you find it?" Lane asked curiously.

"It's parked across from one of my team member's apartment."

"You think that was deliberate?" Lane asked the obvious question and Jax spun back to face Blake's apartment building. There'd been no sign the place had been ransacked, but maybe whoever was there didn't want to leave any traces behind.

"I don't know. It's possible, I guess. Can you let me know what you find out once your lab has a chance to process the vehicle?"

"Sure will," Lane assured him.

"Good. We'll talk soon."

Jax ended the call then climbed back into his car and drove away before patrol cars responded to the report of a man waving a gun in the area. His gut assured him he'd barely peeled back the first layer on the truth. Something bigger than a stolen vehicle was going on, and it was all somehow connected to Blake's death.

Someone was deliberately trying to set up his team, and the suspects were numerous. Al Hasan was believed to have some influential people on his payroll. Was someone from the Afghan Embassy dirty, or were the stolen vehicle, the evasive response from the embassy's driver, and the ambassador's lack of cooperation a fluke? Jax couldn't believe that was so.

Heading home, he took extra precautions, making sure he wasn't being followed. In the growing darkness outside, he was too keyed up to sleep. There'd be plenty of time on the plane. So many disjointed thoughts coursed through his brain. Were they walking into another setup that might prove far worse than the one that took Blake's life?

Chapter Five

Headlights flashed across the front of her dark house. Erin grabbed her weapon and slipped to the window, parting the curtains. Jax's car rolled to a stop in her drive. She breathed out an enormous sigh of relief, feeling it down to her knees. She'd been on edge since realizing she was being followed the day before. What Jax had told her about the Suburban matching the same description as the one following her earlier was alarming.

The knock on the door had her jumping, even though she knew who it was. Erin pulled it open and braced herself to face her commander. He stood before her. Tall. Handsome. Jax.

"You didn't have to pick me up," she said and held the door open wide. He came inside and closed it.

"I thought we could ride in together. No need to take two vehicles." In other words, he was worried about her.

Erin smiled at his consideration. "I'm almost ready. Want some coffee?"

He nodded and poured himself a cup before surveying the place, his gaze finally landing on her.

"I'll go grab my backpack," she told him when those piercing eyes became too much. She hurried to her bedroom and closed the door, blowing out a breath. Her nerves a wreck, she was terrified by the upcoming mission. Unsure if she was up to the task at hand. Add her growing feelings for Jax to the mix, and she was a mess.

Lord, please help me. I need Your guidance. We need Your protection, she prayed, then grabbed her backpack and glanced around the room one final time. Would she come home again? Her thoughts drifted to Blake once more. She believed he'd had an inkling when he left his apartment before that final trip that it was his last mission. Life was short. Fragile. With the type of work they did, there were no guarantees.

Erin returned to the living room where Jax waited. He took her backpack from her and glanced at her injured wrist. She'd removed the brace.

"How's that feeling," he asked.

"Much better. Almost back to normal."

Jax nodded without saying a word.

"We should probably be going," she murmured and clicked off the coffee pot before washing it out.

Jax waited by the door as she took one final sweep of the place before stepping out into the early morning, praying that they'd all return home safely this time.

* * *

The plane touched down inside Bagram Air Force Base in Afghanistan. From there, a Black Hawk would fly them to the staging location.

Once the plane taxied to a stop, each agent disembarked. They were met immediately by the Black Hawk's pilot. There would be no downtime. The drone footage that Peter had shown the team to make the story convincing was vague, and Jax believed most of them knew there was something off about this endeavor. Still, no one voiced their concerns.

Jax had received the coordinates for the location of the first fake mission. An abandoned school. He'd gotten Sam alone and let slip their destination. He felt like a heel for doing it, but he had his orders and was determined to prove his unit's innocence.

"Agent Murphy?" The pilot asked, glancing around at the team members.

"I'm Murphy." Jax stepped forward and extended his hand to the Air Force officer.

The man shook his hand. "Squadron Commander David Arnold, sir. I'm to chopper you and your team to the staging point." Arnold's gaze met his. The commander only knew the details of his part in the mission, for security purposes.

"Thank you, Commander. We're ready to go when you are."

"Roger that. Follow me." Arnold headed toward the waiting Black Hawk. Jax didn't miss the questioning looks among his team members. He hated this.

Jax shielded his eyes against the debris the powerful blades kicked up as he climbed onboard after Erin.

The flight would take less than an hour. Everyone on board believed they were heading out on a mission designed to bring down the illusive terrorist known as Al Hasan, the man the CIA believed responsible for Blake's death. Only Jax knew the truth, and it tore at his gut.

As the hatch closed, each team member found a seat and donned headsets. Seconds later, the commander lifted off and banked hard, heading toward the tall mountains.

Beside him, Erin watched him closely. She knew him well, especially since over the past few weeks they'd gotten closer. She could tell something was up although he'd tried to cover his unease during the entire flight to Afghanistan.

"Are you okay?" she whispered, touching his hand briefly.

Jax nodded, avoiding eye contact. "Yeah, I'm okay. Just trying to wrap my head around what must be done."

He didn't have to look at her to know she didn't buy it, but she let the matter go. "You think he's really the one behind all of this?"

She was talking about Al Hasan. They knew next to nothing about the elusive tribesman. While a nomad, Al Hasan mostly stayed close to the mountains they were nearing. Rumors circulated that he was training the next wave of terrorists and moving weapons into Afghanistan for who knew what possible scenario. Nothing about that could be good.

Jax wished he could talk to Blake's asset himself and find out what he knew, but the man was a ghost. As far as Jax understood, no one knew the name of the man or how to get in touch with him. Peter's claims of speaking to the asset was all part of the ruse.

"I don't know. I sure wish we had more to go on." He glanced at her, and, right away, worry replaced his doubts. "You doing okay? I know this is hard." Her flinch was not lost on him.

"I'm fine. You don't have to keep worrying about me," she told him. "I want to catch this guy. Alive. We need answers about what he's planning. What he's done."

Jax couldn't tell her that none of those answers would be coming from this mission. Frustration seared his mind. They should be hunting down Al Hasan for real. Instead, he was leading his people on a wild goose chase.

"Hopefully, this time we'll get him and figure out what he's planning," he murmured without much emotion.

Erin appeared satisfied with the answer and turned away while he stared out the window as the chopper ate up the territory. In the distance, the mountain range rose against the sky. Every mile that disappeared behind them felt like a clock ticking on their lives. If they failed to uncover the mole before it was too late, everyone's life could be in danger.

Emotionally, he was running on empty and needed a distraction. He reviewed the things he was supposed to do the following day. The fake mission was to take place in a small village in the shadow of the mountains. An abandoned school the target. They'd head out before dawn. Once they were close to the location, he'd tell the rest of the team about their destination.

Jax closed his eyes, trying to rest, but he hadn't been able to sleep in days. Too many dangers rattled around in his head. He couldn't get the reaction of the ambassador's driver out of his head. The man had been hiding something, he could feel it. Was the vehicle really stolen or was that the cover story? Someone was worried about what their team might find out. A prickle of uncertainty seeped into his body. How did the driver of the SUV fit into what had happened to Blake?

"We're five minutes out," the commander announced. Jax roused himself and gathered his backpack. Glancing around at his fellow agents, he noted their serious expressions.

The chopper kicked up dust and debris in its wake as it touched ground with a jarring thud.

With the blades still whirling, Jax opened the hatch. The first to disembark, he ran for the tree coverage close by where Kabir waited for them with a Humvee for transportation. They'd find a secure location to make camp and then head out the following morning.

Erin hopped out next, followed by the rest of the team. Dylan, the last man out of the chopper, closed the hatch.

The pilot didn't wait for Dylan to reach the trees before lifting off. Banking hard left, he was in and out in a matter of minutes.

This part of the country was known as no man's land for a reason. The military had little control over what happened here. The unit had been here many times in the past, so it didn't throw up any red flags that they were back in the war zone. The ruse certainly appeared legitimate enough from the solemn expressions on his teammates' faces. They'd follow him into whatever dangerous situation he led them. Jax hoped he wasn't leading them into a firefight that would cost them their lives to prove what he already knew in his heart.

Chapter Six

"What was that about?" Erin demanded, her eyes spitting fire. She could feel color staining her cheeks. They'd risk their lives coming here and for nothing. The village was almost deserted. Only a handful of old-timers remained. The cobwebs hanging around the school indicated it had been empty for a while, probably years. There was no sign that Al Hasan or any other threat had been in the area. Their intel was bogus.

Jax's lips clamped together as she stormed into his line of vision, forcing him to make eye contact. Instead of answering, he turned on his heel and left the schoolhouse. Her anger spiraled out of control. Erin couldn't let it go. She charged after him.

The rest of the team, including Kabir, whom they'd met at the staging site, slowly followed them out into the blinding sun.

"Jax? What's going on?" she demanded, his reaction more frightening than anything.

He grabbed Erin's arm and pulled her out of earshot of the rest of the group before answering. Frustration simmered below the surface. "Don't ever question my orders in front of my team again." The words seethed from his lips.

Erin refused to back down. "Then explain why you sent us out on a farce. That's an empty school building. Has been for a while. This village is pretty much deserted. Al Hasan certainly hasn't been here recently, if ever." Her voice rose over that last part, emphasizing the words.

Something was wrong. Erin could see it in the way Jax refused to meet her eyes.

She'd become an expert at reading people, even someone as hard to read as Jax Murphy, who'd become notorious for keeping his emotions locked away from everyone. But as they'd grown closer, she'd become familiar with every little look. When his brows slanted together, he was analyzing a suspect or a problem. The lift of one corner of his mouth meant he was thinking about something funny. When his jaw set in a vise-like grip like it was now, only a muscle clenching to give it away, something was clearly wrong.

"We were acting on our intel that said Al Hasan would be here. You saw the drone surveillance photos."

Erin didn't believe what he was telling her. "Those photos showed an unusual amount of activity around the village and nothing more. It could have been herdsmen moving their sheep to greener areas." She turned back to the village and waved a hand. "Look at it. There's nothing going on in there but a bunch of blowing sand." She stared him right in the eye. "But I'm guessing you knew that already, didn't you? So, what's this really about?"

He wouldn't meet her eyes. "I don't know what you mean. Come on, we need to pull out before we're discovered. Obviously, they knew we were coming and moved out." He started past her. "This is getting us nowhere, and we're wasting valuable time."

Erin grabbed his arm, holding him there. "Jax, talk to me. Please, tell me the truth."

He shook his head, his eyes wintery. "I can't." His voice lowered. "Not here. Not now." He glanced at the team, and she let her hand drop.

Fear swirled through her body. She'd been right; something was wrong. Struggling to keep her misgivings inside, she wanted to make him tell her what he knew, but she dropped the matter for the moment.

Jax joined the rest of the unit, who'd watched their exchange with interest. "Tyler, call it in. Let's get moving. This one's a bust."

They headed to the Humvee stationed behind an outcropping of rocks several miles from the village. Erin's thoughts churned. If Jax had known Al Hasan wouldn't be here, why had they raided the village and searched the school? What was he expecting to find?

The dawning of truth sent her gaze jerking toward him. His profile tense, Jax stared out the window without saying a word. The raid was a fake. A test of some sorts? Someone higher up was calling the shots. Did they suspect one of their own of being a traitor? The thought settled around her uncomfortably. Why? There had to be evidence to back up such a horrific claim. Were they all suspects? Something ugly was in the works, and she wasn't sure she wanted to know the answer to any of those questions.

They headed back to the location where they'd made camp, the occupants of the Humvee unusually silent. Jax looked as if the weight of the world rested on his shoulders and she reached out and grasped his hand, entwining her pinky finger with his. He turned to face her, brows raised, surprised by the intimate gesture. A hint of a smile touched his lips. If only she could reach over and brush that lock of hair from his forehead. Assure him everything was going to be okay, but she couldn't do any of those things because she had a feeling the real test had just begun.

Promise me, if anything happens to me, you'll get out of this. You'll leave the CIA. I don't want you to do this without me. Blake's words came back to haunt her. Had she waited too late? Did Blake have some type of premonition that someone close to them was dirty? She shivered at the implication and the fear wouldn't go away.

Father, please hold us. I don't know what we're facing, but I think it's bad.

They drove the rest of the way to camp in silence, yet she still held onto Jax's hand. She wasn't so sure if it was because of his need or her own.

Once they reached camp, the team members exited the Humvee and waited for answers. Had they come to the same conclusion as Erin?

"You think the intel was wrong?" Sam raised the question everyone was thinking. The rest of the unit's focus zeroed in on their leader.

Jax did his best to keep a lid on the unrest. He shook his head. "It was a solid lead. Somehow or other, Al Hasan must have gotten word that we were coming and evacuated."

"With all due respect, Jax, the intel was wrong," Dylan interjected. "I spoke to a few of the remaining villagers. They confirmed no one but a few herdsmen grazing their sheep had been around until we showed up. Al Hasan certainly wasn't there."

Jax whirled on him. "I doubt they would tell you if he had been. Everyone's too frightened of retribution to give him up. Our intel was good," he stressed to the entire team. "Al Hasan was there. We missed him. We can't give into doubts. It's important to stay united." He forced a smile. "Why don't you all get something to eat and then catch some shuteye? As soon as I know what our next assignment is, I'll brief everyone."

After exchanging puzzled looks, the men moved away, leaving her and Jax alone. Erin's heart went out to each of them. They were frustrated. On edge. Running into a situation like the one at the village was a major letdown.

Jax spared her a brief look, then headed into the main tent, no doubt to call Peter and explain what happened.

The thought of food sickened her. Too much turmoil swirled around inside her. The adrenaline rush of the mission had kept her nerves on edge. Right now, she needed exercise more than nourishment, yet she didn't dare venture too far away from camp.

This part of the world was a dangerous tightrope. The Afghan government had little control here. Being from the US instantly put a target on their heads. Few people trusted them. Half the area was ruled by tribal law, while the other was under some type of terrorist oppression.

Boys in particular were forced to participate in "the cause". If they didn't, the entire family's safety became at risk.

Erin headed for an outcropping of rocks a short distance from camp. There was shelter from the sun there, and she needed to clear away her doubts. But mostly she wanted to go to Jax and demand he tell her what was really going on, because the nervous ball in her stomach told her this went much deeper than Al Hasan's assumed crimes. She was beginning to doubt everything she knew about this war.

Being back in the same country where Blake had lost his life had her spooked. She saw ghosts of him everywhere. They'd worked so many missions together side by side, some near this same area.

That final mission was always close at hand whenever she thought about him. Blake's edginess before they'd left. His begging her to get out if anything happened to him. It was almost as if he'd had some premonition he wouldn't be leaving Afghanistan alive.

Frustrated, she shook her head, shielding her eyes against the glaring sun. For the first time, she actually considered Blake's request. She'd been with the CIA going on five hard years now. She'd seen things that haunted her at night, sometimes even into the day. The war seemed to be going on forever with no end in sight. How many more soldiers would lose their lives? How many more of the people she loved?

Still, the thought of walking away from the job made her sad. With no close family of her own, her teammates were her family. If she left, she'd be walking away from the people she considered family . . . and away from Jax. He lived for the Agency, for the missions abroad, for the hunt to bring down a killer before it was too late. It was in his blood. If she left, their contact would end as well.

As much as she wanted to deny it, her feelings for Jax had shifted. After spending so much time together, it was inevitable. Was it real? Or because he was there for her when she'd been at her lowest?

Try as she might, she couldn't get their kiss out of her head. When his lips touched hers, it took everything inside her not to respond. Not to go into his arms and hold him close. It would be so easy to give her heart to him. But while he cared about her, she wondered if he had simply given into a whim when he kissed her, fueled by their shared grief. She was so screwed up inside she could no longer tell if she was reading too much into the relationship. Her heart told her that Jax had been there for her because they had one thing in common. Blake.

* * *

"The game is over. Repeat, the game is over." Peter's message came through the line loud and clear, conjuring up a wealth of questions in their wake.

What on earth was up? An eerie feeling of déjà vu slithered up his spine. Darkness had descended on the camp. Jax's nerves were on edge. They were a matter of hours away from heading out on the second fake mission when he'd gotten Peter's call.

"Copy that." Jax tossed the mic on the makeshift desk and rubbed his hands over his eyes. They were being called to stand down. Something was off.

Since he'd received his orders from the secretary of defense, he'd been intent on following through with them despite the cost, even if the thought of betraying his team ate at his gut. Now, he'd learned that the fake mission tonight was being scrubbed. He didn't like the feel of it. Neither would the team, he could almost guarantee. Especially Erin. She seemed to be on a single-woman mission to locate Blake's killers, and she knew something was wrong with the earlier mission.

Lord, I hate the lies. Please help us bring this thing to an end soon. His disjointed prayer filled the silent space, with no answer in sight.

Jax stepped from the tent into the blinding desert heat. The team was scattered around the camp. Some read magazines. Others cleaned their weapons. He sought Erin out from among the team members. She was talking quietly to Dylan. As always, looking at her sent shockwaves through his body. He'd never felt so torn before. His growing feelings for her made him vulnerable.

"Listen up, everyone," he announced, and all eyes shot to him. Seconds later, the team was standing around him. No doubt expecting answers he couldn't give.

"Tonight's mission is a scrub." He glanced around the group. A mixture of shock, relief, and doubt haunted their faces.

"Why? What's up?" Tyler voiced the question they all wanted to know. "First, the bad intel this morning, and now tonight's mission is off? Something's going on. You must know more than what you're saying."

Jax wished he had a better explanation to give his team. "I'm sorry, I don't. I have no idea why the mission was scrubbed. Maybe another intel breach, like earlier." He lifted his shoulders. Against his will, his gaze went to Erin. He could read her thoughts easy enough. She didn't believe anything he was saying.

Tonight's mission would have been the second fake mission he'd been enlisted to guide his team through. Dylan was the target tonight. Jax planned to leak the location to him shortly before he'd gotten the call from Peter. So far, the plan to draw out the traitor had failed miserably.

"Sorry I don't have more for you, but that's all the intel I'm privy to at the moment. Hopefully I'll know more later on."

Leaving the team to their assumptions, he ignored Erin's attempt at drawing his attention. He couldn't have the discussion she wanted right now. He needed to talk to Peter. Alone.

Jax returned to his makeshift command center. Before he could call Peter, the sat phone beeped.

"Murphy." He could hear the strain in his tone.

"It's me." Peter's voice came through clear enough for Jax to hear the concern. "Are you alone?" Even through the static on the line, something in Peter's voice warned him this was going to be bad news.

"Yes. Is the line secure?"

"Affirmative," Peter confirmed.

"I need to know what's going on, Peter. My people have questions. Why was the mission scrubbed?" Jax's frustration bled into his tone. He wanted to get all the lies over with and return to the task of bringing down Al Hasan.

Peter heaved a heavy sigh into the receiver. "Something's happened." He paused before adding, "Something big."

Jax's blood ran cold. It was a couple of seconds before he could bring himself to ask, "Like what?"

The silence on Peter's end didn't bode well. "Hours ago, we received some very disturbing intel. That's the reason tonight's mission was scrubbed. This is critical, Jax. I need your unit deployed tonight to a different location . . . and I'll meet you there." Those words confirmed Jax's worst fears. "This is not another drill. This is the real thing."

"Okay," Jax said at last. "What are the coordinates?"

Peter didn't answer right away. "I need you to keep the location confidential. We can't afford a screw up here. Our intel has been verified. Something big is in the works. There's a training camp nestled in a valley some distance from the Mendiu Pass. We believe it's where Al Hasan is camped out. We hit it tonight. I repeat, no one can know about this, Jax, not even Erin. The last thing we need is another disaster like what happened with Blake."

An uneasy feeling slithered down Jax's spine. He blew out a breath. "Okay. What do I tell my people?"

"Tell them the mission is back on, but nothing more. Once I'm onsite and we're a go, I'll announce the details to the team." Peter gave him the coordinates, then added, "Good luck."

Luck. Jax would need more than luck to see this through. He needed divine intervention, and he planned to ask for it. But, first, he needed answers. "What aren't you telling me?"

His commander's sigh carried volumes. "I'm afraid it's bad. We've had a team combing through every member of your unit, tearing their lives apart. Phone records. Associates. Finances." He stopped. Drew in a breath. Announced the worst news possible. "We've found something."

Jax could almost feel the blood drain from his face. Why didn't Peter spit it out? "What?" he prompted, his tone irritated.

"An offshore account with a quarter of a million dollars in it. Jax, it's in Erin's name."

The revelation almost took his knees out from beneath him and sucked the breath from his body. An offshore account in Erin's name? Impossible. He couldn't get the words to compute. Erin was intense. Driven. Passionate about her beliefs. She was all those things. What she wasn't was a traitor. Nor did she care about money.

"No way. Someone's setting her up." The reality of what Peter said made it impossible to keep Jax's anger from showing.

"I'm inclined to believe you, but the evidence against her is hard to dispute."

Jax couldn't believe what he was hearing. "Well, we have to try. Erin's one of us, and she needs our help. *We* have to help her."

"What do you think I'm trying to do?" Peter snapped. "I'm doing everything in my power to find out the truth. But the fact remains, Erin has to be considered a suspect until we can prove differently."

Jax understood that truth, but still, he couldn't imagine Erin in that role. "How long before you have to share this with Director Dean?"

Peter took his time answering. "A few days. I can't keep a discovery like this secret for long. Sam was the one to uncover the account before you deployed. I've asked him to keep it to himself for a while. He'll honor my wishes for now out of respect for both Erin and Blake, but we can't sit on this long."

"I understand. What can I do to help?" He couldn't believe Sam had held onto information this big without sharing it with him. Jax's thoughts shifted in a dozen different directions. Why would someone want to frame Erin for Blake's death? Something more was going on here, and he had to find out what it was before it was too late.

"Keep your eyes open and your opinions unbiased. If she's guilty, she's guilty. If not, the truth will come out. Stay safe. I'll see you soon." Peter ended the call.

Jax still held the phone in his hand. He didn't care what evidence they might have dug up; he'd never believe Erin was capable of such a horrific thing. Yet if someone with this much juice was trying to frame her, then finding the real person behind the crime was going to prove a difficult task.

When he couldn't stand his own company any longer, he went outside. "Listen up," he said and garnered everyone's attention immediately. "We have new orders. The mission's back on. We leave at 0300 hours. Get some sleep."

Stunned silence followed. Frustration covered their faces. His people didn't know what to make of the newest command. Unfortunately, he couldn't enlighten them. Jax stepped away before they could ask any questions.

He needed to talk to Erin. Needed her to help ease his concerns. He glanced around, but she had disappeared.

She stood away from the camp in the shadows of the rocks near the ridge they used as camouflage. She looked like she wanted to be alone. But he needed answers.

"What are you thinking about?" he asked when he drew close. She swung to face him. He'd startled her. His lips turned up into what passed as a smile. "Sorry, I didn't mean to scare you."

This was the part of the job every agent hated the most. The waiting. You'd spend hours—even days—sitting around trying to keep from going out of your mind with boredom, waiting for orders that would send you into a firestorm of danger. Thinking about the possibilities of what awaited them was as agonizing as it was endless. He'd take boredom any day.

Erin placed her hand over her heart. She'd looked so lost when he came upon her that he shoved aside his worries about the mission and the charges mounting against her.

"No, it's okay," she said at last when she'd accepted him into her personal space. It was no small feat. Erin was naturally a private person. Blake was one of the few people able to get her to open up to him. Not so much for Jax. But then, he was the one she turned to with her grief. That had to mean something.

"I was thinking about that last night. You know, before . . ."

He understood what she meant. In hindsight, that night had been fraught with warnings. If only they'd been looking. Jax reached over and clasped her hand, entwining their fingers. "I know."

As he peered into her eyes, one thing became clear. He was crazy about her. If only he could foresee a happy ending for them. He prayed for the strength to let her go gracefully when the time came.

She didn't move away for a moment. As always, whenever he was close to her, he wanted more. Wanted what she couldn't give him.

Erin pulled her hand from his and faced him head-on. He let her go reluctantly, knowing what was coming next. "What's going on? The mission this morning felt off from the start. Almost as if we were playing a game."

Jax glanced back at the team. A few had bedded down for some much-needed rest. Some sat around talking quietly.

He'd been sworn to secrecy, yet he knew he'd tell her everything . . . except the allegations being formed against her. He couldn't even think about those horrible lies. "That's because it was a setup."

She stared him down, trying to make sense of what he said. "What do you mean a setup?"

He tugged her further from the camp. The night was pitch-black. The sky full of stars above. No moon yet. With the exception of the cloud cover, it could have been the night before Blake's death.

"I mean there was no sightings of Al Hasan. It was all a setup."

Erin blew out a breath. "Why?" she asked incredulously.

He took his time answering. "Because it's believed that someone on our team has been leaking confidential information to Al Hasan."

Jax was inches from her. He could almost feel her reaction before he spotted the wide-eyed shock on her face.

She stared at him for the longest time before shaking her head. "That's . . . impossible. These people are like family. And Blake was the one who brought Kabir in. He trusted him implicitly."

When Jax didn't answer, Erin's gaze narrowed, her voice raised slightly. "Wait, are they saying Blake might have been dirty?" His silence answered her question. "That's ridiculous. He's dead, for crying out loud."

Jax's gaze shot to the people around the campfire, then back to Erin. "I'm telling you that, right now, no one is beyond suspicion."

"Where's this coming from?" she asked in a shocked tone.

He'd been sworn to secrecy. But she had his heart.

"Tell me, Jax. Is it Peter?" She probed him with her gaze. He'd given something away. Or maybe she'd become good at reading him. "Higher?"

He slowly nodded, confirming her hunch. "This is from the Pentagon. The secretary of defense delivered the news personally before our last briefing stateside."

Erin stepped away, putting more distance between herself and the camp. He followed.

She whirled back to him. "This is crazy. Isn't it? Tell me it's crazy. There's no way any one from our team is dirty."

Jax had argued the same points to no avail. "I know that, and so do you, but I have my orders. Until everyone can be cleared, we continue on with the fake missions."

"What happens when everyone is cleared? Are they going to try and sweep this whole thing under the rug or lay it at Blake's door?"

He wished he could answer no, but his gut was pointing him in a different direction. "I don't know." He blew out a sigh. "I honestly don't know."

"What about tonight's mission? You sounded different when you mentioned it just now. Is it real?" She knew him too well.

He nodded. "Yes, it's real. Peter called it in. He sounded . . . worried. This one's important." And he had a bad feeling about it.

After a silent standoff between them, she moved closer. His heartbeat went ballistic as usual. He was crazy about her, and it was getting harder to keep his feelings to himself. If only she felt the same way about him.

Jax shelved that argument for another time because her eyes darkened and she stepped closer. He drew her into his arms without resistance. Felt hers circle his waist. They stared into each other's eyes for the longest time before he lowered his head, his lips claiming hers. All the while, his heart wished for so much. For the war to end. For life to return to normal. For Blake to still be alive. For Erin to return his feelings.

She kissed him back with the same reckless abandon he felt swirling inside. The kiss deepened. All thoughts disappeared but the woman in his arms. He lost himself in her gentle touch.

When she pushed against his chest, it took a moment before he realized what was happening. His eyes flew open. Seeing the uncertainty in hers, he reluctantly let her go. Erin turned away. Her breathing labored like his.

"I'm sorry," he said, but didn't feel sorry. Anything but. "I shouldn't have done that."

She didn't look at him. "We should go back. The others will miss us." She brushed past him without as much as another word, and he let her.

Her footsteps faded away, and he closed his eyes. Foolish. He'd behaved foolishly. It was imperative that he keep his focus on what lay ahead tonight. His gut told him they were heading into a violent situation, and it was going to take all their wits to come through it alive.

He felt so lost. Desperate for help that could only come from one place, he closed his eyes and prayed, pouring out his heart to God. When he'd finished, a sudden breeze kicked up all around him, then returned the desert to its former peace. If only he could find the same for his aching heart.

Chapter Seven

Enemy territory

0300 hours

The unnerving silence inside the Humvee spoke of the gravity of the mission. Everyone inside felt it. No one said a word.

Outside, the night was pitch-black. Titanic clouds blotted out the stars and moon. The coverage would work in their favor to a certain extent. The element of surprise would be on their side, but reaching their destination through the rugged terrain in such blackness could prove fatal. Keeping their movements secret, even amid the vast desert, would be impossible. Enemy combatants roamed this area.

Peter's presence confirmed the seriousness of what they were doing. They'd been deployed to a target location deep within the foothills of the Hindu Kush mountain range bordering the porous pathway into Pakistan. They were armed with few details and no military backup. Another indicator of the severity of this mission. Secrecy was critical.

Jax sat next to Erin, his arm touching hers. She found it oddly comforting in spite of the tension she could feel in him. Reaching for his hand, she held it. She couldn't not care about him.

It had been almost five weeks since the ambush that ended in Blake's death, yet even now, his death—being back—felt surreal. She still expected to see him every time she walked into CIA headquarters in Langley. She could almost picture him seated next to her now. Cracking dumb jokes to ease the tension.

Her heart tattooed an unsteady beat against her ears. She wished she could think of something to say to help ease Jax's mind—hers, everyone's—yet her brain was a blank, while her gut practically screamed warnings to her.

Kabir pulled the Humvee behind some rocks. They'd be covering the last two miles on foot. In this part of the desert, the mountains worked as an amphitheater. Sound carried for miles. They couldn't afford to alert the enemy they were coming.

"Let's go, people. Everyone keep your eyes and ears open," Peter ordered in a terse voice and then exited the Humvee. The unit fell out after him.

Jax turned to her with that same expression on his face the night Blake died, and her stomach clenched.

He whispered, "I don't like it, Erin. Something's not right. Stay close to me. I don't want to lose you too." Normally she would have argued, but something about this mission didn't feel right to her either.

"If you see anything out of the ordinary, sound the alarm right away," Peter said in a low voice.

They spread out in small groups. Jax and Erin taking the lead. They were in enemy territory.

For the past hundred feet or so, they'd been steadily gaining altitude. In these foothills, the temperature had plunged at least twenty degrees in half an hour. They tried to keep as quiet as possible. Erin felt alert like an owl, glancing in all directions.

As they continued their upward climb, the altitude played havoc with her breathing. She sucked in breaths but couldn't seem to capture enough air in her lungs.

Once the unit summited the final rocky hill standing before them, Jax took out his night vision binoculars and panned the area below. He focused on one particular spot. Erin did the same, quickly seeing what he was looking at. Their target. A compound nestled in the valley between two rugged mountains. There was no sign of life below. Nothing stirred. Had the camp been deserted long ago, or had someone tipped its occupants off?

Erin's uneasiness increased tenfold. She thought about what Jax said about the secretary of defense's accusations that one of their team was dirty. The fake mission they'd worked earlier. She stared at the quietness below them and realized Jax was right. Something about this whole thing felt off. Where was Al Hasan? His men?

Al Hasan first emerged on the CIA's terrorist watch list a few years back. It wasn't long before he'd reportedly became one of the deadliest men around. It was suspected that he was training dozens of troops and moving massive amounts of weapons into the country at an alarming rate, yet there was no clear picture of him available anywhere. A vague surveillance photo had been captured a few years back when he first appeared on their radar. It showed a man dressed in traditional clothing with little of his face visible. He looked like so many other men.

"Listen up," Peter ordered. "We go in silent and fast. Intel has close to a dozen of Al Hasan's men training here. Possibly more. We don't know what we'll find inside those tents, people. Dylan and Tyler will enter from the northeast side of the camp. That's where the drones have the field ops set up, so you shouldn't run into any resistance, and that'll hopefully get you into the camp undetected. Sam, myself, and Kabir will enter from the south. Erin and Jax, you take the east end. Once you're all in place, we go on my command."

Peter glanced around at the faces before him, his expression drawn. Troubled. They'd performed this type of mission half a dozen times or more. The timing was down to perfection, but something about the rush to get here worried Erin. "This one's important," Peter reminded them. "We don't know exactly what we're getting into down there, so stay alert and stay alive. Let's go."

They descended the hill with stealth. One by one, the team acknowledged their position with a short whistle. Once everyone was in place, Peter signaled with another longer whistle. The silent count went to ten and then they were in motion.

Erin and Jax eased with caution inside the camp. Nothing stirred. The place appeared eerily silent. In the past, they'd always run into a certain amount of opposition, which they managed to disarm. It came with the territory. The fact that they'd practically waltzed into the place undetected was another sign something didn't feel right.

To their left, a large tent had been erected. No doubt used for meetings or possibly a makeshift mess hall. Beyond that, three slightly smaller tents served as sleeping quarters for the troops.

In a matter of minutes, the rest of the team converged in the center of the compound. Each shook their head, indicating they'd not run into any enemy troops.

Peter pointed to the three smaller tents indicating that Dylan, Tyler and Sam should search two while Peter and Kabir took the third. Jax and Erin would cover the larger tent.

He watched as his team entered their respective tents, then he and Erin headed toward the back side of the larger shelter.

"I don't like it," Erin whispered, her voice shaky. She glanced over at Jax. His expression was drawn. His gaze darting around them.

"Me neither. This isn't right. I'll go in first. Keep a watch out for anything unusual."

With his weapon drawn, Jax stepped inside. A few seconds later, Erin followed.

He stopped halfway inside the tent, whirling to face her. It was his expression that first told her something was dreadfully wrong. He looked as if he'd seen something frightening.

"What is it?" she asked, her heart hammering against her chest.

She just got the words out when he yelled, "The place is wired with explosives. Run, Erin." Jax grabbed her arm and they raced toward the opening as fast as they could. They barely made it ten feet from the entrance when the earth around them rumbled and shook, then exploded with unparalleled shockwaves.

* * *

Dust boiled in all directions, covering everything.

Erin! Where was she?

He stumbled to his feet. Fear pumped adrenalin through his body at a rapid rate. He'd lost visual of her during the explosion. The tent and everything inside was reduced to a pile of rubble in a matter of seconds. Panic slithered down his spine. Reality set in. They were supposed to be dead.

His hair was matted with blood, and he was scraped and bleeding in several places, but he was alive and in one piece. He ignored his pain. All he could think about was finding Erin. As the dust began to settle, he spotted her lying in a crumpled heap a few feet away. He ran to her side.

Please. Lord. Let her be alive.

"Erin." Her right hand lay at an awkward angle. The same one she'd injured before. The blast had embedded bits of shrapnel in her face. Jax shook her hard, and she opened her eyes. "Are you okay? Can you move?"

Before she could answer, a series of explosions rocked the earth beneath them once more. The remainder of the tents went up in a firestorm of blaze and smoke. Had the others escaped before the explosion?

Jax covered Erin's body with his until the immediate danger passed. They glanced at the raging inferno that replaced the tents. Jax grabbed his radio. "Dragon Team Two, this is Dragon Team One. Come in."

Empty silence met the request. He looked at Erin before repeating the command. "Dragon Team Three, come in. Dragon Team Two, come in." He shoved the radio back in his jacket pocket and helped her to her feet.

If his people had been inside the tents when the blasts occurred, they wouldn't have survived. He shoved the doubts aside. "Let's search the explosion area and pray they're alive. Stay close to me." He shot her a glance. "We don't know what we're facing. Whoever set the explosions could be close."

Jax hurried to the last place he'd seen Peter. Fire blazed from the contents of the tents, scorching his face. Shielding his eyes, the truth became apparent. No one from their team had made it out alive except for the two of them.

He glanced around the wasteland. "We need to leave. It'll be dawn soon. The people responsible for this will search the area for any survivors. It won't take them long to realize we got out."

Emotion clogged his throat and he couldn't choke back the grief. He was shell-shocked. They'd lost five good men in a matter of minutes. All were friends. No one deserved this.

Jax forced his chaotic thoughts to come together. No matter how much he hurt and needed to grieve, now was not the time. The people responsible for this much destruction would stick close by to see the results of their work. They'd check each corpse. Every bit of evidence remaining. He and Erin had to keep moving.

He swiveled to face her. Erin cradled her wrist against her body. Agony and grief marred her face. There was no time to address either.

"We can't go back the way we came," she said. "Whoever set us up has probably destroyed the Humvee by now. They'd want to get rid of any evidence we were ever here."

They cleared what was left of the compound and were now faced with a decision. "There's only one way out of here," Jax said and spun toward the dark monster looming behind them. "We'll have to cross over those mountains."

Together they stared up at the silhouette of the mountain range that had been the backdrop of some of the bloodiest battles in the War on Terror.

Crossing the mountains meant they'd be facing dangerous weather conditions, including freezing temperatures. Yet the greater threat was traveling further into enemy territory. The passage here between the Hindu Kish Mountains was a known terrorist route. Right now, who posed the greatest threat? Al Hasan, the enemy they'd been tracking for years, or the traitor from their own country responsible for the carnage they'd escaped?

"It's our only hope of staying alive." He stopped and peered at Erin. His heart went out to her. She had no way of knowing that her own people believed she was a traitor. The discussion he'd had with Peter all but confirmed that reality. If he had any say in it, she never would. He'd do everything within his power to prove her innocence.

"Are you up to it?" he asked gently, seeing the pain etched on her face.

She drew in a breath. The injury to the same wrist was an excruciating reminder of how difficult the crossing would be. "I am, but shouldn't we call this in first? Let Coleman know what happened?"

Erin glanced over her shoulder, surveyed the damage, then swallowed visibly. She'd loved each of their fallen comrades as well. The loss was indescribable for her as well as him. Jax couldn't imagine the torment their families would go through when they learned the truth.

Unable to stop himself, Jax faced the death trap they'd narrowly escaped before he shook his head. "Right now, our survival depends on staying ahead of whoever is responsible for what happened here." He avoided her intense look and started walking, knowing she'd seen what he'd been trying to keep from her.

Erin caught up with him quickly. "You know something more, don't you? What aren't you telling me?"

When he ignored her question and kept walking, she grabbed his arm and stepped into his direct line of sight. "Jax?"

He tried to think of something believable to satisfy her curiosity. "Truth is, I don't know who to trust. Whoever was responsible for this knew we were coming. They wired the place expecting to kill everyone who walked into those tents. We're all supposed to be dead. Why? Why are they coming after us full force?"

Erin stared him down, trying to make sense of what he said. "There's something more you haven't told me."

The lack of moonlight made it hard to read her expression clearly. Jax moved closer. The death of his team weighed heavily on his conscience. He'd sent his friends to their death. "I'm saying, someone with intimate knowledge of this mission—someone from *our* side—tipped them off."

Erin blew out a breath, and they started walking once more. "There's no way." She felt as strongly about the team's innocence as he once had. "I refuse to believe it was someone from our unit. It has to be someone else. Someone with a lot of juice, to be able to pull off an attack of this magnitude."

He was inches from her and could almost feel her trying to make sense of what he'd said. Glancing sideways, he focused on her face. She was wide-eyed. Shocked.

"This is crazy. Isn't it? Tell me it's crazy," she said, breathing the words out.

Jax had argued the same points to himself, to no avail.

"So, what happens now that everyone's gone and we're still alive? Are they going to try to lay the blame for what happened at our door?"

He wished that he could answer no, but he knew the truth. The secretary of defense had cleared him already. He wasn't under suspicion. Erin was the one they were coming after full force. He tried to come up with a decent answer for her. "I honestly don't know. Right now, we need to try to stay alive long enough to clear our names and figure out who's really behind this. So can you make the climb or not?" The words came out harsher than he intended. He was angry, not with her, but with the person responsible for so much carnage.

Erin wanted to ask more, he could tell, but now was not the time.

She slowly nodded. "Don't worry about me, I'll be fine." But he had his doubts. He couldn't help it. He could see the way she favored her wrist. It was going to be a struggle to summit the mountain.

"Wait here. I'll see if I can find a decent place to cross." Jax left her alone, needing to gather his composure. He couldn't let her see how worried he was. Their entire team was dead. Their friends gone. Someone close to them had set them up. And the CIA's top suspect was Erin.

Nothing about the path they'd have to take was reassuring. It would be a rough trek, but they were out of options. He shook his head and went back to her. "Here." She jumped when he materialized beside her. "Sorry," he said and took off his jacket. Ripping parts of the liner out, he wrapped her swollen wrist tight, then he tied a piece of the cloth around her neck in a makeshift sling. "Better?" he asked.

"Yes, much. Thanks." She attempted a half-hearted smile, putting on a brave front, but not fooling him for a second.

"That should keep it from jostling around too much as you walk. I'm afraid there's no easy way over the mountains, though."

Erin was a trained agent. They'd been through situations like this before. She'd pull her weight. With a final look behind them, she shivered and said, "Let's get out of here."

She followed him to the path he'd chosen. When they reached it, he stopped. "Without proper climbing gear, there's really only one way over." Nothing about their crossing would be easy, but at least it wasn't a sheer upward climb. There were enough rocks and small scrub trees to help with the footing, and it would give them something to grasp.

On the other side of the mountain range lay Pakistan. Jax wasn't sure which was the lesser of two evils. Staying and facing a traitor who'd killed his entire team or summiting that mountain range. He prayed they weren't signing their death certificates by crossing into a territory where it was rumored the price of a life could be bought and sold to the highest bidder.

Chapter Eight

Erin couldn't hide the throbbing pain in her wrist. It had swollen to almost double its size. Even with the wrap and sling, every little move sent pain shooting up her arm.

"Let's stop for a second," Jax said when he saw that she was in trouble.

Erin nodded because managing a single word was impossible. Exhaustion weighed down her limbs. They'd been walking nonstop for hours. She dropped to a large rock, closing her eyes briefly. It had been daylight for a while. With the sunrise, every step they made now posed a potential threat.

Taking out a canteen, she drank conservatively. Jax did the same, glancing around their surroundings. He was worried for good reason. She could see the tension in his shoulders. The taut set of his jaw.

Pulling her thoughts together was next to impossible. Their entire team had been slaughtered. They were on their own like deer during hunting season. She couldn't wrap her head around it. By now, the people who'd set the explosions knew they were still alive and would come after them. She and Jax couldn't afford to rest for long.

"How's your wrist holding up," he asked, moving closer to her.

Truth was, she was barely hanging on, but she couldn't tell him that. He had enough to worry about. "It's okay." She tried to sound positive, but fell short, and he saw it.

Frustration sparked in his eyes. "We need help. There are more of them than us. We'll be outmanned if it comes to a firefight, and they're highly motivated." She knew what that meant. If they were captured, they'd be as dead as the rest of their team.

"I'm going to try Coleman on the sat phone. See if he can get us out of here."

Erin nodded without answering, conserving her waning energy. She tried not to get her hopes up. Even if Coleman could arrange to get them out of the area, they'd still have a lengthy hike in front of them.

Jax stepped away, searching for a good signal. When it finally came, he dialed the number. Her eyes glued to him as she said a silent prayer for God's help. She didn't want to die here with so many unanswered questions.

"Coleman, thank goodness. It's Jax. We were attacked." Relief swept through her as Jax explained what had happened. "I have bad news." Jax paused. "Everyone else in the unit was killed, including Peter. Erin and I managed to escape, but we need your help. The people who set the explosives are still out there. We need an exit plan." He stopped to listen, his gaze latching onto Erin.

"Yes, I believe so, but I'm not sure how much longer we can stay hidden," Jax answered. "This is dangerous territory, as you well know. The enemies are unlimited, not to mention the weather playing a factor. We won't stay alive long under these conditions."

She shivered at his words. The clouds from earlier had begun to produce snow. With the flurries, the temperature had plunged to below freezing.

"I understand." A frown creased Jax's forehead. "You're kidding? I can't believe it." All color seeped from his face. Something was wrong. "Okay," Jax breathed out, then typed something into his burner phone. "I have the coordinates. We'll be there."

He ended the call, then ran a hand over his eyes.

Erin jumped to her feet and went to him. "What is it?" she asked, fearing his answer.

He blew out a sigh. "The weather's preventing an immediate extraction. They're going to try to get us out tomorrow afternoon, if the weather clears. We'll meet them at an abandoned airstrip across the border in Pakistan."

The news wasn't good. They'd have to hike all day and through the night to make it to the site. She studied his face. There was more.

"What haven't you told me?" she asked.

His gaze fell to hers. "There was an attack late last evening on the Afghan ambassador as he was heading home."

Shock left her speechless for a moment, her eyes wide. "Is he okay?"

"I'm not sure. The embassy isn't talking, but I sure hope so. Coleman and the ambassador are friends. They've known each other since they worked together following 9/11. He's pretty torn up about it."

Erin tried to make sense of the latest news. How did it play into what happened here? "Do you think the ambassador's attack is related to this?" She swept her hand around them.

"I don't know, but I'd say it's a pretty odd coincidence, wouldn't you?" He shook his head. "We still have a lot of miles to cover before we get to the location, but the good news is: help is on the way. Someone else knows what happened here."

He touched her face gently, and she closed her eyes. His words sounded like pure heaven, as did his touch.

She leaned into his hand, feeling warmth and strength there.

When she opened her eyes, he was staring at her with a strange expression on his face. She'd seen it so many times before. It lay bare all the longings of his heart.

Swallowing visibly, he drew her close. Her eyes grew large, looking into his, seeing things that gave her hope and made her want to run away at the same time. He leaned in, his lips against hers. A tiny sigh escaped as she lost herself in his kiss. Her hand rested on his chest as the kiss deepened, and she found herself drowning, blocking everything else out, including the fight to live that lay in front of them.

But they couldn't stay in this tender moment long.

Jax slowly ended the kiss, his eyes dark with emotion. Questions she couldn't answer there. She leaned her head against his. She just wanted to be close to him for a little while longer.

"Erin," he whispered her name. She knew he wanted to talk, but she wasn't ready to go there yet. Couldn't let herself think about the future with so much uncertainty facing them.

She shook her head, touching her finger to his lips. "Not yet. I don't want to talk about it yet."

As she peered into his eyes, she could tell this was not what he wanted to hear, but he accepted her answer for the moment.

He draped his arm around her and tugged her into his embrace. It was the two of them against an unknown enemy. Their future was as dark and frightening as the journey facing them and the nightmare they'd barely escaped. It didn't do to look beyond the moment. They had much to overcome to survive, and, if they did, she had a feeling there would be even more obstacles waiting for them.

Thinking about the future now was futile when there was no guarantee either of them would have one.

* * *

Jax reluctantly let her go. "We should keep going," he said without looking at her, his tone distant, unable to help it. Her rejection was like a knife to the heart. Jax was well on his way to falling in love, yet he had no idea where he stood with her. He shook off the dark weight of hopelessness with difficulty. Facing the grueling journey ahead of them was going to take all his wits. He couldn't afford to engage in the emotional warfare going on in his head.

Even though she tried to be strong, he could tell Erin's wrist was giving her trouble. Her face was drawn, her eyes glassy. He'd packed first aid items in his backpack. Jax dug out some pain meds and handed them to her. "It's not much, but it'll help with the pain," he said gently.

She smiled. "Thanks." She took the pills and washed them down with water.

Above, dark clouds threatened to engulf them as did the dropping temperatures. Light snow continued to fall. More was on the way. They'd need to find shelter once the weather moved in, but for now, they had to keep going because Jax had a feeling the men who had set the trap for his team would track them relentlessly.

"Who do you think is really behind this?" Erin asked, forcing him to shove aside his troubled thoughts for the moment.

Jax shook his head. "I don't know, but I'm beginning to think this may not be the work of Al Hasan at all. Maybe someone's trying to lay the blame for these attacks on him." He glanced sideways at her. "Someone with intimate knowledge of how we do our job."

He had her full attention. She said, "It can't be anyone from our unit. They are all dead . . ." She stopped walking and faced him, reality dawning in her eyes. "Am I under suspicion?"

It wasn't in him to lie to her. No matter how much it hurt to speak the truth, he slowly nodded.

The shock on her face was easy to read. She swallowed. It was a long while before she could force the question out. "What do they have on me?"

He couldn't keep this from her any longer. "They found an offshore account with a quarter of a million dollars in it." He hesitated a second. "Your name is on the account."

Her hand flew to cover her mouth. "That's not possible," she managed in a whisper.

Jax wished he could make it better for her. "I know that. Someone is obviously setting you up to take the fall for everything. The only question is who?"

The fear in her eyes shook him to his core, and he clasped her uninjured hand. "We'll get to the bottom of it, I promise. I'm not going to let them frame you for something you didn't do."

A hint of a smile touched her lips. She squeezed his hand, then let it go. "Thank you."

"You're welcome." Keeping his feelings to himself with her close and looking so vulnerable was next to impossible, but he pushed them down. That was for another time. Right now, they had to stay alive long enough to find the true killer.

Ahead of them lay an endless vista of rugged terrain and hidden dangers. They were without options. Going back meant certain death.

Jax glanced around them. "Let's head out. Our only chance at staying alive until our team arrives is to keep one step ahead of the enemy."

He started walking again, and she kept up with him despite her injuries. Erin would do everything in her power to carry her weight.

As they continued their upward trek to the top of the pass, Jax scoured the unfamiliar countryside, unable to dispel the feeling they were being watched.

The snowfall turned heavier with the predicted storm moving in. How long before they'd have to seek cover? Under these conditions, not long. Although he was exhausted to his core, he couldn't relax. Trouble loomed everywhere. Since Blake's death, they'd all been struggling to understand the reasons behind it. Now, the rest of his unit was dead along with his direct commander and good friend, and they were no closer to discovering who was behind the attacks than they were the night of Blake's death.

He kept his eyes trained on the wooded area surrounding them, unable to shake the feeling that Al Hasan had been served up as a scapegoat to cover the true terrorist's identity.

The lack of details concerning the presumed terrorist should have been their first clue. Haashim Al Hasan appeared to be in his early thirties. According to Blake's asset, he was the son of herdsmen, who grew up in a small village near this very area. Not much to point to the man as a possible terrorist, really. What if everything they believed they knew about Al Hasan was a lie?

Out of the corner of his eye Jax thought he saw something. He stopped suddenly, squinting at the dense treed area to his left. Was that movement close by?

Erin halted next to him. "Do you see something?" She barely got the words out when more than a dozen armed men emerged from the trees around them.

Dressed entirely in black *Payraan Tombaan,* with *lungees*—or turbans—covering their heads, they moved closer. Jax whirled around. The men were everywhere. He and Erin were surrounded.

"Drop your weapons," one of the men ordered in the Dari language. Jax's blood ran cold. Who were these men?

"We're outnumbered. What do we do?" Erin whispered, her voice less than steady, her full focus on the men advancing on them.

There was only one choice if they wanted to live. "We do as they say." He slowly lowered his Assault Rifle to the ground in front of him. After a moment's hesitation, Erin did the same. With his heart pounding in his chest, he waited to see if they would kill them in spite of their cooperation.

A single man hurried forward and grabbed both their guns, then fell back in rank.

Once they were unarmed and vulnerable, the men closed ranks around them, stopping but a few feet away, weapons trained on them without saying a word.

A frantic prayer sped through his head. They needed God's help, and now, if they stood a chance at living.

Seconds ticked by in silent standoff. Jax's breathing became shallow, his pulse racing. Were these the men responsible for killing his team? Blake? If so, then what were they waiting for? Why not finish them off while they had Jax and Erin at their mercy?

His answer came swiftly when another man pushed through the circle of men. Shock rippled through Jax's limbs. Was it possible? He recognized him! Though the only image they had of the man had been flawed, Jax was almost certain this was the man they'd been chasing for several years now. The supposed terrorist known as Al Hasan.

Erin involuntarily moved closer to him. His gaze sliced to her. She looked as if every drop of blood had left her face. She'd figured it out as well. Had they been wrong? Was Al Hasan responsible for the attacks after all? If so, then how did the man obtain his intelligence? How would he have known they were raiding his training camp in the middle of the night? The thought was unsettling.

Like the rest of his men, Al Hasan was dressed entirely in black. The man stopped a few feet away, eyeing them both with open suspicion. When he spoke, he addressed them in fluent English. What he had to say about cut Jax's knees out from underneath him

"What is the CIA doing in our land?" Suspicion and open hostility showed on the man's face.

Jax's gaze shot to Erin. The same shock rippling through him was there on her face.

Al Hasan knew they were CIA. What else did he know?

Jax fought past the questions swamping him. If captured by the enemy, they were trained to deny being part of the CIA. "I don't know what you're talking about. We were hiking and got lost in the storm."

The man's lip curled into a smile at Jax's answer. "You are CIA," he said without emotion. "Why else would you be here in this dangerous part of the country? Certainly not on a hiking trip. So I will ask you again, why are you here in my land?"

Jax had no idea how this encounter was going to play out, but something about the man didn't add up. His gut told him this was no criminal mastermind like they'd been led to believe.

"We came here looking for you, Al Hasan," he told the man. "And it looks like we've found you."

"An honest spy. That must be a rarity." Al Hasan's smile widened. "And why would you be looking for me? I am a humble herdsman. I'd say you have far more serious things to deal with. And if what happened back there is an indication, you're looking in the wrong direction. I suggest you focus on someone closer. Someone from your own organization perhaps."

Jax's brows slanted upwards. Al Hasan's accusations mirrored his and Erin's beliefs. "What do you know about that?" he asked.

Al Hasan's expression returned to blank. "I know everything that happens in my country. Just as I know you lost many of your own men back there, and you are being followed. If they catch you, they'll kill you as well."

Jax felt as if his shock was frozen on his face. He couldn't believe what he was hearing. "Followed by whom? You're the only one I see following us."

Al Hasan shook his head. "Unlike you and the CIA, I mean *you* no harm. I only want what's best for my people and my country, and that doesn't include your people, serving your own agendas, interfering with that. Your country has done enough damage to ours. Villages wiped out. Families displaced. Dead. So many lives lost. Your war has left Afghanistan ravaged for years, and it is no closer to being over than it was in the beginning." He drew in a breath and let it go. Then he motioned to the man who had taken their weapons. The man came forward and handed the weapons back to them. With a nod, Al Hasan and his men turned to head back up the mountainside.

Stunned, Jax shoved his weapon into his jacket pocket and went after him. One of Al Hasan's men blocked his path.

"Who's following us? If you know something, help us," Jax demanded, his tone reflecting his frustration.

Al Hasan glanced to the man blocking Jax, then the man backed away.

Facing Jax, he said, "Why should I help you? Your people have branded me a terrorist without a shred of evidence. They've forced me to live on the run with my family. There's a bounty on my head and on the heads of my people when it's your own who are the true evil ones." He shook his head. "I'm afraid I cannot help you." With those chilling words, Al Hasan turned and covered several steps before stopping. He stood still for a moment, then turned back to Jax once more.

"The storm is coming in quickly. Out in the open up here is no place to be, even for a spy. Our camp is past that ridge." He pointed up ahead. "You can ride out the storm there with us. We have food and a warm fire. Once it passes, you must do what you believe is right."

Chapter Nine

Al Hasan turned and began walking again. He and his men slowly picked their way up the mountain with the ease of those who were used to trekking through rough terrain.

"What do you think that was about?" Erin forced the question out, fear still pumping through her veins. She and Jax stood planted where Al Hasan had left them, watching as the men disappeared.

Jax pivoted to face her, his eyes wide. "I don't know, but if this man really is the hardened killer we've been led to believe, he would have murdered us right where we stood and thought nothing of it."

"But can we trust him?" She was filled with doubts, unsure whom to believe. She was being framed for Blake's death and probably what happened to their team today. Someone close to her was spreading lies, soiling her reputation, while they'd been led to think Al Hasan was the true enemy.

Above them, lightning lit up the countryside, chased by an enormous clap of thunder. With her nerves shot, Erin jumped in alarm. Thunder snowstorms were a rarity. This one appeared to be building up momentum.

Jax caught her eye. "Right now, I'm not sure who to trust, but facing this nasty storm while exposed and vulnerable isn't exactly a welcome idea. I don't think we have a choice. We need to go with them."

When she didn't answer, Jax grabbed her good hand and together they followed Al Hasan and his men.

Once they crested the ridge, the men headed off to the right and further into the woods. Erin hesitated. Still holding her hand, Jax looked back at her, his brows raised in question.

She shook her head and followed. The twilight of the forest made it hard to see. The storm intensified, and the snow came down thick.

Just when Erin was beginning to worry they were being led to their deaths, she spotted what appeared to be an opening in the side of the mountain. A cave. Nothing about it looked inviting.

Al Hasan and his men disappeared inside. Once they reached the opening, she stopped and faced Jax. "Are we making the right decision?" she asked, wishing Jax appeared more confident.

He shook his head. "I don't know," he answered honestly. "But what choice do we have?"

Still holding her hand, Jax entered the cave. Off to the left, one of the men waited for them. When he spotted them, he headed down what appeared to be a long passage without a word. After another glance exchanged, they followed.

When they'd traveled a short way, the passage ended, opening into a large circular room. A fire burned brightly in the middle. Dozens of men, women, and children milled about.

Al Hasan motioned them over to the fire. Every molecule in Erin's body screamed they were making a huge mistake by trusting him, yet their choices were limited to stay and risk being wrong or leave and end up at the mercy of the elements and whoever was responsible for taking out their team.

Erin lowered herself to the ground near the fire. Jax hesitated briefly before doing the same.

Across from them, Al Hasan dropped down with ease. A woman brought food to them. Erin recognized the meal immediately. *Kabuli pulao*, a dish that consisted of steamed rice with chopped raisins and carrots served with lamb. The woman poured strong black coffee and handed cups to them. Then she hurried away, her face filled with mistrust.

"My wife. You must forgive her. She doesn't trust Americans. Her entire family was killed by a drone attack a few years back. Our only child died as well."

Shocked, Erin stared at the woman who had returned to a group of women. She couldn't imagine how hard it must be to lose a child like that. Certainly, she couldn't blame the woman for not trusting them. "I'm sorry," she murmured and realized how trite her apology sounded.

Al Hasan snapped his fingers. One of the men standing nearby hurried over. He spoke to the man in a low voice. Erin couldn't make out what was said, but the man rushed away. A few minutes later, he came back carrying something and advanced toward Erin.

"That's far enough," Jax immediately rose to his feet in a protective gesture.

"He means you no harm," Al Hasan told her. "Basar has herbs that he has made into a salve to help ease the swelling in your wrist."

Erin visibly relaxed. Basar knelt next to her and opened a folded cloth that contained a small bowl with a pungent-smelling paste inside.

Basar pointed to her wrist and set the paste down near her. With Jax's help, she removed the makeshift bandage. The swelling was severe. She could barely move her hand.

Taking some of the paste from the jar, Jax gently smeared it around her wrist while Erin bit her bottom lip to keep from showing the excruciating pain the simple gesture caused. Once he'd finished, he rewrapped her wrist, and Erin placed her hand back into the sling Jax made for her.

"Thank you," she told Basar, who bowed his head, then moved away.

The rest of Al Hasan's men stood some distance away watching them with the same distrust his wife had shown.

"The storm should pass in a few hours. You must leave once that happens. I can't risk having you give our location away to your people who are coming to rescue you." Al Hasan paused. "I hope you don't regret letting them know you are still alive."

Erin flinched at his words. Even Al Hasan was convinced their own people had betrayed them. Her gaze slid to Jax. She could see the same doubts there.

"How do you know our people are coming here?" Erin asked, keeping her full attention on the man.

Al Hasan shrugged. "After what happened to the rest of your team, I'm sure you contacted them right away. They'll be here soon enough." Al Hasan leaned forward, his gaze intense. "But you are warned, not every CIA agent's motives are what you believe them to be. That attack earlier wasn't led by any of our people. That was all you."

* * *

"The storm is winding down," one of Al Hasan's men informed him.

Al Hasan nodded, then turned to them. "You must go now. We must break camp soon, before the people responsible for the earlier attack find us and you. The weather has kept them immobile, but now that it is clearing, they'll return to the hunt."

Jax couldn't dispel the feeling that Al Hasan knew more about the attack than he was saying, but it would be futile to ask any further questions. Al Hasan had refused to answer their questions so far.

With nothing left to do, Jax and Erin gathered their backpacks and headed for the cave's opening. Al Hasan went with them.

"If you keep on the path you were traveling earlier, you should summit the mountain before dark. The temperature will drop drastically with darkness, you'll need protection from the elements. Once you reach the top of the mountain, head to your right. You'll see another small cave there. It will provide shelter for the night. Do you have the means to make a fire?"

"Yes, we have a lighter," Jax said.

Al Hasan nodded. "There should be enough dead trees around to use for fuel. Good luck to you both. I hope you find the answers you are looking for."

Jax had never felt so frustrated before. There was something more in the works here than either he or Erin understood, yet, from Al Hasan's stony expression, he knew it was pointless to press him for answers.

Al Hasan handed Erin a small jar. "Basar wanted you to have this. Keep applying it to the wrist. The swelling should go down by morning."

Erin nodded, then with a final wave, Jax and Erin headed out of the cave.

Al Hasan gave one final warning. "Be careful, agents. You have to suspect that if your own people took your comrades' lives, they won't hesitate to do the same thing to you. You could be walking into a trap." Before Jax could formulate a response, the man turned on his heel and disappeared into the bowels of the cave.

Outside, the storm had dumped several inches of fresh snow on the ground. At any other time, the setting would appear peaceful, but, with Al Hasan's warning still ringing in his head, peace wasn't on Jax's mind.

After they'd put a little distance between themselves and the camp, Jax voiced his concerns. "He seems pretty convinced this whole thing was a setup created by our own people." He studied her profile. All his doubts were reflected in the taut set of her face.

"And he knows more than he was willing to say. I think he saw who set those explosives. He knows who killed our people."

Frustrated, she shook her head and faced him. "His conclusions aren't anything that we haven't already thought of ourselves."

Jax nodded, then searched the path ahead of them, looking for trouble. "I hate feeling as if I'm working in the dark." He blew out a breath. "If someone from the CIA is involved in this, Al Hasan could be right. We may be walking into a trap tomorrow. I trust you and Coleman. I don't trust anyone else. While Coleman can be a bear to work for, he's the only one we can count on to get us out of here." He glanced at her uneasily. "If someone has been feeding both Peter and Coleman incorrect information about you, then what else has been fabricated?"

Erin nodded. "The truth about Al Hasan for one. He's not a terrorist. He's being set up as well." She scanned their surroundings. "What do we do? We can't wander around here until we figure out what's really going on. Yet if we don't make the meet, we might not get out of here alive. Who knows how many people are hunting us down? We'll be lucky to make it to the meet location."

He'd thought the same thing, but sought to reassure her. "We'll be careful. We won't go near the site until we're sure it's safe. If anything seems off, we leave and call Coleman to figure out our best plan of getting out of here. Do you have a map of the area?"

She nodded. Pulling it from her backpack, she handed it to him.

Jax spread it out on a rock, his mind reeling. Trying to grasp where they were and the direction they'd need to travel once they reached Pakistan was next to impossible.

They'd been walking for several hours, all the while Al Hasan's warning kept niggling at his brain. If they were heading into a setup and the men hunting them tracked them to the airstrip, then there would be no escape. He was more than a little worried. The people responsible for killing their entire unit had proven they were good at covering their tracks. Spreading lies.

Jax struggled to keep his concerns to himself. "Let's see if we can find the place Al Hasan told us to hole up for the night. It's getting colder by the minute. We can rest for a while and then figure out our best route."

He couldn't let go of the helplessness building up inside him. His mind kept going over what happened at the camp earlier that day. They'd walked into a carefully laid trap. The killers expected them. They knew exactly when they'd arrive. The explosives were set ahead to go off soon after they'd breached those tents. No one was expected to walk out alive. How had the killers known the CIA was coming? The details of the mission were kept confidential for the agents' safety. Unless someone from inside had tipped them off.

"Over there," Erin said.

His eyes followed where she pointed. In the gathering darkness, he could make out a black hole against the side of the mountain.

Relief lightened some of the load he carried. "Let's get going. I can't feel my feet anymore."

They hurried as quickly as their weary bodies allowed.

Jax stopped Erin before she went inside. "Hang on a second. We don't know what we'll find in there. Let me take a look around first." He dug out his flashlight and clicked it on. "I'll be right back."

She grasped his hand, keeping him there. "Be careful," she murmured, the look in her eyes tugging at his heart.

"I will," he promised. She let him go, and he headed inside the cave. This one appeared much smaller than the one where Al Hasan and his people had encamped.

A passage greeted him. He headed down it, the flashlight's beam bouncing off the stone walls. He'd only gone a short distance when the passage ended, opening up into a space barely four foot in diameter. If the people following them came across the cave, he and Erin would be in imminent danger, but at least they'd be out of the weather for the time being.

He returned to where Erin waited. "There's not much room, but it's dry and out of the cold."

"Sounds like heaven right now," she murmured and followed him inside. Once they reached the room, she glanced around. "Do you think we can risk a fire?" She shivered from the cold, her teeth chattering.

"I think we'll be okay as long as we conceal the entrance. I'll go get some firewood and then cover the opening. You should take a load off. That wrist must be giving you grief."

She took off her backpack and dropped to the floor, barely managing a nod.

Jax was worried about her. He went outside and gathered as much firewood as he could carry, then took it back inside and dumped it on the ground before returning to hide the entrance with brush.

When he returned, he dug in his backpack and found the lighter. Stacking the wood close to where Erin sat, he gathered some dried brush to use as kindling. Once the fire was going, he knelt next to her. "How's the wrist?" he asked.

She smiled at him. "Believe it or not, it's doing better. Whatever was in that ointment that Basar made seems to work. I put some more on it just now. The swelling appears to have gone down quite a bit."

He returned her smile and scraped a strand of her hair from her face. "I'm glad. You should try and get some rest. I'll stay awake for the first watch. I have a feeling we're going to need all the sleep we can get to face what's coming our way tomorrow."

Chapter Ten

Something woke her. With her heart hammering in her ears, Erin shot up, her eyes darting around the small space. As her vision grew accustomed to the darkness, she realized Jax was nowhere around. She stumbled to her feet. Where was he? The fire had almost gone out, though the cave was still warm.

Erin headed for the entrance when someone slammed into her. She froze and tried to pull away. Her eyes filled with terror.

"Hang on, Erin, it's just me." Jax clutched her arms, concern on his face.

"You scared me. I woke up and you weren't there," she said trying to calm her pulse.

"I'm sorry. I didn't mean to worry you. I went outside to take a look around."

She drew in a couple of breaths, her heart rate slowing. She focused on his expression. Something was troubling him. "Is someone out there?" she asked.

Jax shook his head. "No, and that's just it. Where are the people who set the explosions? We've seen no sign of them."

She searched his face, her thoughts spinning. "You're right. The only person we've encountered is the one person we're supposed to be hunting."

"I don't like it," he said.

It didn't make sense in her mind, and she could tell he felt the same way.

"If they were sent there to kill us all, they wouldn't have pulled out without making sure that was accomplished unless . . ." She stopped. "The call to Coleman. Jax, what if they intercepted it somehow?" She shivered at the implication.

"If that's the case, they'll be there waiting for us at the meet site. It won't be good."

His gaze latched onto hers. "We have to warn Coleman. The extraction team could be in danger as well."

Jax went to his backpack and took out the sat phone. "There's no signal here. I'll go outside and try again."

Erin followed him. She glanced around the desolate area while Jax made the call.

He turned to her. "He's not answering."

Worry sped up her spine. "What if the real person behind this figured out what Coleman was trying to do and . . ." She couldn't finish. The thought of their call putting the director in danger was terrifying.

Jax drew in a breath. "Let's not jump to conclusions. He may not be able to take the call. Let's go inside where it's warm. I don't think it's wise to be out here in plain sight for too long."

She hurried to the cave and waited while Jax shoved brush in front of the opening. Once inside, he piled more wood on the dying fire.

"I'll keep watch for a while," she told him.

He came over to where she stood, his gaze piercing. Her heart strummed an unsteady rhythm against her chest when his arms encircled her. Her hands rested on his chest as he gathered her close, his lips claiming hers.

She couldn't help it, she melted against him and returned his kiss with all the growing love in her heart. She cared for him. Wasn't sure how it happened, but her feelings had changed, and she didn't want to hide them any longer.

Erin closed her eyes, losing herself in his kiss. Jax felt like the future she longed for, and that scared her.

He pulled away, peering into her eyes. He wanted to talk. But what was there to say? She had no idea if they would even survive this mission, and if they did, she was done because she couldn't keep doing this anymore. She wanted out. Wanted more than living in the shadows. So where did that leave them?

Reality swept between them and she turned away, touching a trembling finger to her lips. She'd given in to emotions that had no place in this dangerous country. "You should try to get some sleep. It'll be daylight in a few hours," she murmured.

He said nothing and moved away. When she turned, he'd lain down on the ground, facing away from her.

Erin struggled to let go of the regret. She couldn't handle this with so much at stake, but she knew sooner or later they'd have to have a talk about what was happening between them.

Soon, his breathing grew even in sleep. Erin sighed deeply, then sat close to the fire and tried to bring her troubled thoughts together.

It felt as if she were suspended in a perpetual state of disbelief. Today, they'd lost so many good men, and they still had no idea what was going on. Whoever was behind the ambush had gone to great lengths to annihilate their entire unit. The same people were trying to frame her for their crimes. How did the money get into an offshore account under her name?

How many more lives would be lost before the truth came out? She glanced over at Jax sleeping close by. She cared about him and couldn't bear to think of losing him.

Now, more than ever, Erin craved God's presence, His comfort. She closed her eyes and whispered a prayer under her breath. "We need Your guidance, Father. We don't know where to turn or who to trust. Nothing is as it seems. Please, help us." The only answer was the crackle of the fire and the faint breathing of the man sleeping nearby who'd occupied a lot of her thoughts lately.

*　*　*

Someone shook him. His eyes flew open. Erin knelt next to him, worry on her face.

He sat up quickly. "What is it?" he asked.

"I heard footsteps outside," she whispered. "More than one person's."

He jumped to his feet. Grabbing the rifle, he followed her to the entrance and listened.

She was right. Someone was out there who spoke Dari. Thankful for the language training he'd received, Jax tried to decipher what the man said.

"They've been here," an accented voice said. "Search the area. This time they cannot get away. Too much is at stake."

Erin's gaze locked with his. "What do we do?" she whispered. They were sitting ducks tucked inside the cave.

Their only hope was the element of surprise. "You go over there, and I'll stand on the opposite side of the entrance. Once they enter, we take them." Her eyes grew large. He could tell she understood the longshot facing them. They had no idea how many men were searching for them or how heavily armed they were. But if the two of them wanted to stay alive, it was their only chance.

Erin nodded and moved into position while Jax edged close to the entrance and flattened himself against the stone wall.

Lord, we need You, he prayed. It felt as if it were he and Erin against the world, fighting for their lives.

Footsteps, more than one set, moved outside the cave. A rustling noise followed. They were removing the brush Jax had placed in front of the entrance. Would they guess it was placed there deliberately?

Jax's gaze sliced to Erin. She nodded, her expression taut. Uncertainty reigned in her eyes.

A man entered, followed closely by another. The two men barely had time to take a few steps before Jax and Erin sprang into action.

Jax grabbed the man closest to him wrapping his arm securely around the intruder's neck before the guy could call for help. The man struggled and flailed, trying to free himself. Within seconds, he grew limp in Jax's arms. Jax lowered him to the ground, then rushed to Erin who had her gun trained on another man. With the butt of his rife, Jax clocked the man hard in the temple. He dropped to the ground at Erin's feet.

Jax grabbed rope from his backpack and secured both men's hands and feet, then he gagged them.

"We need to leave. Now," he whispered. "We don't know how many more are out there, and it won't be long before the others come looking for these two."

Shouldering their backpacks, they eased out of the cave and recovered the entrance. The storm had deposited additional snow during the night, but it wasn't enough to cover the tracks Jax had made, which had led the men to their location.

He glanced at the ground, as did Erin. Footprints covered the place. There had to be more men searching for them. Escaping with their lives would be difficult.

Jax pointed toward the direction they needed to go. "We have to be as quiet as possible," he mouthed.

She nodded, and they picked their way through the forest, both on full alert and expecting another attack at any moment. Once they'd put some much-needed space between themselves and the men searching for them, Jax took out his binoculars and panned the area.

"I don't see anyone," he told her and handed her the binoculars.

She peered through the lenses. "I don't either, but we know those two weren't alone. Maybe the rest of their unit is further down the mountain."

"Possibly," he said with doubt. Before he got the words out, the countryside exploded with the noise of gunfire. Multiple shots exchanged. Barrel flashes lit up the area below.

"I count at least a dozen shooters." Erin's brows shot up. "They're shooting at each other." She handed him the binoculars, and he surveyed the gunfight below.

"That's Al Hasan's people on the left. They're firing on at least five armed men who appear to be retreating." Jax lowered the glasses. "Al Hasan saved our lives."

Erin stared at him. "And someone has been trying to set him up too."

"The only question is who and why?" He watched the action below. Al Hasan's people continued their attack. It wasn't long before the attackers were dead. But there were two men who might shed some light on what was really going on.

"We need to go back," Jax told her. "Get those two men in the cave to talk."

She nodded, and they hurried down to where Al Hasan's men were searching the pockets of the dead men.

When Jax and Erin entered the area, the men whirled on them, weapons drawn.

"Whoa," Jax held up his hands as he approached. "We're not with them."

"Lower your weapons," Al Hasan ordered, and his men quickly obeyed.

Jax and Erin approached where Al Hasan stood.

"Do you know these men?" Jax asked.

Al Hasan nodded, his dark eyes revealing little. "I do. They are mercenaries. They sell their services to the highest bidder. Unfortunately, they are all dead."

Jax shot Erin a look before answering. "Not all of them. There are two in the cave. They attacked us. We need to see what they know."

He started for the cave, but Al Hasan raised a hand to stop him. "They won't talk to you. They fear the people who hired them far more than anything you could do to them. You need to leave the area while you still can. These are not the only ones coming after you. Let me handle these men. If I find out something useful, I'll let you know."

Jax eyed the man suspiciously. "And why should I trust you?" Right now, he trusted Erin and her alone.

"Because I saved your lives and I know these men. They will not talk to you," Al Hasan assured him without emotion.

As much as Jax wanted to interrogate the men in the cave, it was imperative for him and Erin to put distance between themselves and the nightmare trailing them. Jax pulled out his burner phone. "If you find out anything, use this phone to let me know." He programmed in the number for a second burner that Erin carried.

Al Hasan took the phone. "I will let you know, you can be assured. For now, you should get going as quickly as possible because whoever hired these men will come looking for them soon enough to make sure they fulfilled their end of the bargain. When they see this," his hand indicated the men lying dead, "they will know you two are still out there, and they will keep coming. And I won't be able to protect you for long."

Chapter Eleven

"Do you trust him?" Erin asked once they were out of earshot.

Jax peered over her. "Not completely, but he's right. Whoever hired those men won't be satisfied until they know for certain we're dead."

She blew out a breath. The conspiracy was worse than they originally believed. "They killed Blake first. Why? If they wanted us all dead, they could have accomplished it when they killed Blake. What's this really about?"

Jax shook his head. "I wish I knew. So far, I have nothing but questions and no answers."

Erin felt the same way. Why was their entire unit targeted? "Why are they trying to frame Al Hasan for their crimes? This whole thing about a training camp . . . So far, we've found no real evidence of its existence, and from what I can tell, he's not guilty of anything other than trying to stay alive."

"He must have gotten onto someone's radar," Jax said. "They want him gone for a reason. I'm guessing he saw something he shouldn't have, and for that, they're trying to brand him a terrorist."

"I'm sure he trusts us about as much as he trusts most foreigners. I can't say that I blame him after all of this."

Jax glanced up at the sky still heavy with clouds. The brunt of the storm had faded, but snow continued to fall. Maybe it would cover their tracks. "If the weather holds, we should be able to reach the meet location by early afternoon. Hopefully, the extraction team will be there on time, and everything will go according to plan."

She hoped he was right. Because staying alive long enough to reach the extraction site was going to prove a near-impossible task as it was.

"Did Blake ever say anything to you about his asset?" Jax asked her. She knew what he was thinking because she'd thought the same thing. Perhaps Blake's asset was behind the attacks.

"No, nothing. You know Blake. He kept the identities of his assets secret, respecting their need for anonymity."

Jax shook his head. "This is one time I wish he hadn't been so protective of his people. We sure could use the name of the asset who led us on that failed mission."

Erin felt as if her head were on a swivel. She was on alert—they both were. They'd barely escaped a massive explosion, only to be ambushed by mercenaries, and the one person they'd believe to be the enemy had saved their lives. The ball of nerves growing in her stomach seemed to indicate this was only the beginning.

A thought occurred, and she asked, "What did Peter tell you about this last mission? What was so different about it that he felt the need to be part of it?"

Jax stopped for a second to take a breath, look around. "That's just it. He didn't tell me anything. He said the mission was too important to give out details . . ." Jax's gaze slid to her. "He was worried about someone overhearing, I believe."

"So, something huge popped up within a matter of hours. That's why the previous mission was scrubbed. I'm assuming it was another test?"

He nodded, and they started walking again. "Yes. I was told to give the coordinates to Dylan. We were a go, and then, well, you know the rest."

Erin had never felt so helpless before. Nothing made sense and yet everything pointed to someone at the CIA, or possibly even higher up in the chain of command, being involved in the conspiracy against their own government.

"And another strange thing is, in the past, on 'real' missions, we always had a team of marines attached to our unit. Why not this time?" she said, and a chill sped down her spine.

Unexpectedly, the sat phone in his pocket rang. Capturing her gaze, Jax dug it out of his backpack.

"It's Coleman." He frowned, stepping a little away from her.

The action had her wondering why.

Jax spoke briefly, then ended the call and came back to where she stood, a dismal expression in his eyes.

"Something's happened?" she correctly interpreted his look.

He barely nodded. "The meet time has been moved forward. We should still be able to make it okay, but I don't like it." He shook his head. "Coleman made sure that you were still with me. He said I needed to bring you in for your own safety."

"They're going to arrest me. I can't let them do that." Fear coiled through her body, her exhausted brain struggling to come up with a plan.

"I'm not going to let that happen, Erin. Coleman promised me that wasn't the case." He peered into her eyes, and she believed he would do everything in his power to protect her, but would it be enough? Would he lose his life trying to save hers?

"Do you believe him?" she asked, her drawn expression making it clear that she did not.

"I do. He's on your side, I promise. Don't worry."

She shook her head. "I can't go with you, Jax. I can't go to that meet site."

He pulled her close, his gaze so lost. "And I'm not leaving you behind. I can't." Something shifted in his eyes and she sucked in a breath. They'd been trying to stay alive, hunted by an enemy they didn't know, unsure whom to trust. Facing death had a way of clearing away the clutter from one's head. She cared about Jax. She wanted them both to pull through this, but she had no idea what their uncertain future held, or even if they'd walk out of this thing alive.

Erin touched his cheek, then leaned in and kissed him gently then let him go.

Before she moved away, he caught her hand, entwining their fingers. "We'll get through this together. We're a team, and I'm not leaving you behind. We're in this together, no matter what."

* * *

They reached the crest above the extraction site. Almost there. Jax pulled out the binoculars once more and zeroed in on the abandoned airstrip that contained a single rundown building. Nothing stirred.

"I don't see anything," he told her, wishing he felt more confident. "Are you ready to get out of here?" Jax forced a smile. He read all her uncertainties and tried to quash his own. It didn't matter what happened, he'd battle the higher-ups to the death if necessary before he'd let them lay the blame for what happened at Erin's door.

He surveyed the well-traveled path of descent, worn down by years of illegal crossing. It was much too vulnerable and not an option. "Our best bet is to stay in the coverage of the trees until we reach the bottom. We're still in danger. They could be waiting for us down there." He turned to look at her.

She swallowed visibly, then nodded. "Let's do this."

With a final glance below, Jax picked his way down, Erin close behind.

Every little noise had him whirling around, looking for trouble. He couldn't imagine what Erin must be going through, knowing the charges facing her. He understood her not wanting to leave if she was going to be arrested. But Coleman had given his word, and in spite of their differences, Jax trusted the man.

A noise some distance behind grabbed his attention. Were those footsteps? Jax tugged Erin behind the nearest tree and kept her close.

On the traveled path close by, five men dressed in tribal clothing slowly made their way past. They talked amongst themselves. Jax didn't see any sign they were armed, but, after everything that had happened, he wasn't about to take a chance.

He and Erin stood huddled together until the men were well out of sight.

Jax blew out a shaky breath. "That was close."

"Do you think they're part of the group who tried to ambush us earlier?" she whispered so only he could hear.

He couldn't be sure. "They didn't appear armed, but we can't take the chance. We'll give them a wide berth. Once they're in front of us, we can keep an eye on them better."

Jax let her go, and together they eased down the mountainside into Pakistani territory. The men ahead of them appeared unaware they were being followed as they continued to make their way past the abandoned airstrip with nothing more than a few cursory glances.

Once Jax and Erin reached level ground, they stopped. "They don't appear to be interested in the airstrip. Still, we can't take any chances." He took out his binoculars and focused on the airstrip. "I don't see anything, including our extraction team." He checked his watch. "They should be here by now. "

"Should we get a closer look?" she asked, eyeing the building with a frown on her face.

Jax shook his head. "No, we wait for their arrival." He focused on the men. They had stopped now, as if resting, even though the snow continued to fall and they were out in the open. Unease slithered down his spine. He didn't like it.

"Something's not right," he said in a tight voice. "Those men, they're no longer moving."

He handed her the binoculars. She scanned the area, then suddenly grabbed his arm. "There's movement inside the building."

Jax took the binoculars again and zeroed in on the area that she'd pointed out. He saw it too. "I count at least five men inside. There are probably more. Our people will be heading into a setup." Jax grabbed the sat phone and tried to reach Coleman, to no avail. "He's not answering. We have to find a way to warn them."

Erin removed her backpack and dug inside. "I have a flare gun."

Shock and relief warred for control. His brows raised. "You do? That's great," he murmured. "That might save their lives."

As he continued to watch the men, the noise of a chopper could be heard advancing. Erin heard it too. She quickly loaded the flare gun. "I'm good to go," she assured him.

"We need to warn them before they get within firing range."

The chopper cleared the mountainside. Erin aimed the flare gun and fired. The flare shot up in front of the chopper several feet. The pilot immediately banked left and headed back toward the mountain. Seconds later, the area exploded with gunfire.

The chopper cleared the nearest trees. Dozens of men charged out of the building. While Jax watched through the binoculars, he saw something terrifying. "They have a surface-to-air launcher!"

Before Erin had time to answer, the man with the launcher fired on the chopper. As they watched in horror, the missile hit its mark. The chopper exploded in a ball of flames, fiery pieces raining down on the ground, the impact sending shockwaves through the whole area. No one onboard the chopper stood a chance.

"We have to leave. Now. They were expecting us, and they'll come looking," He grabbed Erin's arm, and they turned and raced through the woods. Behind them, men shouted from the airstrip. He couldn't make out what they were saying, but it didn't matter. There was a target on both their heads.

"Hurry," Erin urged as they raced through the wooded area, tree branches snagging their clothes and faces. Jax could hear his breathing over the frantic beat of his heart. Behind them, multiple footsteps advanced at a fast click.

The trees ended, and they descended on a decent-sized village. Jax stopped abruptly. Erin did the same, drawing in several lungs full of breath. A handful of people milled around the area. They'd probably seen the explosion.

"We're going to stand out like crazy here," Jax said. Several people watched them with suspicion in their eyes. "We need to get out of sight now. I don't know where these people's allegiances are. They might give us up to the men following us."

"Over there." Erin pointed to the edge of the village that backed up to wilderness. "If we can make it there, we have a chance."

He and Erin hurried toward the trees without running. No need to call more undue attention to themselves.

They barely reached the edge when the first group of men emerged on the other side of town.

"We have to hide now," Erin urged, and they ducked behind a couple of trees.

From his vantage point, Jax could see the men heading toward the center of the village. "Those guys will question the locals about our whereabouts. If they give us up, we're dead. Our only chance at surviving is to keep one step ahead of those men."

They headed uphill away from the village. The twilight in the forest settled around them. Snow up to a foot in spots made walking difficult, but their choices were nonexistent.

"Do you think those men saw us after the chopper went down?" Erin asked, and he knew what she was thinking. If the men didn't know where they'd gone, then they'd have a better chance at surviving.

"I sure hope not. In any case, we need to put as much distance as we can between ourselves and them. We have to keep fighting, Erin. It's our only chance to stay alive."

Chapter Twelve

They'd been walking for more than an hour when Erin stopped long enough to catch her breath. "I don't hear anyone behind us," she said, peering over her shoulder.

"I don't either. I'm guessing the villagers are more afraid of them than us."

Erin pulled out her canteen she'd refilled and drank deeply, while Jax did the same.

"Why take out the extraction team? They had to realize they'd be calling a whole lot of attention to themselves. Not to mention our people will realize what's happened and send reinforcements soon enough."

Jax pivoted to look in her eyes. "I'm guessing they don't want us to leave here alive, and they're willing to stop at nothing to keep that from happening."

She could see the weariness around his eyes. They'd been fighting so hard to live that they hadn't had breathing room enough to figure out why this was happening to them.

"I'll try to reach out to Coleman again. He needs to know what happened here." His voice sounded full of remorse. Jax took out the sat phone.

Before he could make the call, she grabbed his arm. "Wait."

He stopped dialing and peered into her eyes, his brows raised.

"What if they're tracking our movements by phone somehow? We can't risk giving away our location."

He slowly put the phone away, still holding her gaze. "We'll be on our own."

"I know." She was terrified by that realization, but right now, they couldn't risk another firefight because she wasn't sure if they would survive.

"All right," Jax said and slowly nodded.

Erin dug in her backpack and took out a map and unfolded it.

"Do you remember the location of the safe house in the area?" Jax asked. The CIA had safe houses for their agents set up across most countries. Pakistan was no exception.

Spreading the map out on a rock, Erin scanned it.

"Here." She pointed to the town of Peshawar some distance away.

Their eyes met. "That's an awful lot of extremist territory to cover," he said.

It wasn't ideal, but it was their best bet. "What other option do we have? We can't go back to Afghanistan. It's too dangerous."

He nodded and blew out a sigh. "You're right. We'd better get going then."

Erin refolded the map and tried to put it back into the front pouch for easier use, yet something prevented it from going in. Puzzled, she felt inside the pocket and found an envelope.

Pulling it out, she stared at her name written across the front. She recognized the handwriting. "That's Blake's writing," she said in disbelief, showing him the letter.

"How did it get into your backpack?" he asked, his gaze locked with hers.

Erin shook her head. "I don't know. I haven't opened that compartment in a while . . . Blake must have put it there before our last mission." She swallowed nervously, then handed the letter to Jax, her hands shaking. "I don't think I can read it."

He took it from her and ripped the envelope open. A piece of paper along with a key were inside. Jax turned the key over in his hand. "It looks like it belongs to a safety deposit box. Did Blake ever mention having one to you?" His expression was puzzled.

She shook her head. "Not to my knowledge."

"I found a receipt for one in his apartment before we left on this trip, but there was no key. I guess I know why."

Jax unfolded the letter and scanned it. "Oh no," he murmured, his eyes wintery when he looked at her again.

"What does it say?" She forced the words out in the grips of fear. Something bad was coming.

"I think I'd better read it to you," he said quietly then cleared his throat before he slowly began. "Baby sister, if you're reading this, then I'm dead and I want you to know how much I love you. How important you and Jax are to me. You're my family." Jax stopped for a moment. She braced for what was coming next.

"I did something bad, Erin. Really bad. I can never expect you to understand why, but I didn't feel that I had a choice. They threatened people I love. They threatened you. The key here fits a safety deposit box at Capitol Bank and Trust. It's in your name. Everything that happened, what I'm involved in, will be explained there. It was the safest place I could think of to hide something this important. In the box, you'll have all the proof you need to put the people responsible for my death and others' away forever. I'm sorry, Erin. I wish that you didn't have to see me this way. I wish I didn't have to get you involved in my crimes. Please don't hate me, baby sister. Love always, Blake."

Jax blew out a sigh, his gaze fixed on her eyes as tears welled there.

"What did Blake get himself involved in?" she finally managed. Her heart broke for Blake. She loved him, and nothing he could do would change that for her.

Jax shook his head. "I don't know, but whatever it is, I think it's the reason they're trying to kill us now. Why they killed our entire team. We're collateral damage. They have to keep their identity secret along with their crimes, and they don't care who they kill to accomplish that. They can't let whatever evidence Blake gathered come to light."

She stared at him wide-eyed, her heart aching. "I can't believe it. They killed Blake and so many good men to cover what?"

Jax cupped her shoulders, drawing her into his embrace. "We'll find out the truth, whatever it is. Together we'll find out what set all of this in motion."

She drew in a shaky breath and looked into his eyes. "Thank you," she murmured, brushing a hand over the tears. Her heart was filled with sorrow over losing her big brother in such a senseless way.

Jax never broke eye contact, his expression solemn. "For what?"

"For not believing I'm guilty despite the evidence manufactured against me. For being there for me after losing Blake. I wouldn't have made it through any of this without you, Jax, and I want you to know how important you are to me."

As she peered into his eyes, something shifted in her heart. Her feelings for him solidifying. The future uncertain, they didn't know how much longer they'd have, but she was glad she was spending it with him no matter the length.

She leaned forward. A breath separating them. Uncertainty written all over his face. She understood. Before, she'd given mixed signals. Now, she needed to be close to him. Holding his face, she kissed him, her heart overflowing with emotions she couldn't begin to explain.

A throaty growl came from inside him, and then he was kissing her back, the worries around them temporarily at bay.

When the kiss ended, she could see all the questions in his eyes. She'd hurt him before, and she'd find a way to make it up to him. Leaning against him, she listened to the steady beat of his heart. He was more than a friend. She wanted more from him. But she couldn't let the future's promises take flight just yet.

* * *

Jax cleared his throat. Reality swept back in. "We should probably move out." The words were an unwelcome intrusion between them.

She looked up at his face, then smiled. "You're right. We've got to finish this, find out the truth—for all the people who lost their lives because of it."

He slowly let her go. Glancing at the swollen clouds above them, he feared the weather would continue to play its part in their quest for freedom. "There's more bad weather moving into the area. We're going to need a place to take cover soon."

They started walking again while Jax tried to keep his thoughts on the mission before them instead of on the woman by his side. His thoughts kept returning to her. His heart told him she cared about him. For him, there was no doubt. He was crazy in love with her, but he understood the reasons why she kept him at a distance. The battlefield was the last place to give into your emotions.

He fought the fog of weariness, trying to sort through what little facts they understood. He was in need of a sounding board, and Erin was one of the best. "Do you mind if we go over what we know so far? Maybe we can piece together a clue of what's really happening."

She clasped his hand, squeezed it briefly, then let it go. "Yes, that will give me something to take my mind off how scared I am." She grinned at him.

He stopped walking, entwining his pinky finger with hers. "It's okay to be scared," he said. "We've been through some harrowing moments lately, and the danger isn't anywhere close to being over."

Letting her go, they headed down the route they'd been following once more. "So far, we know that Blake's attack has nothing to do with Al Hasan," Jax said. "But someone is definitely trying to make us believe it does."

"If Al Hasan didn't have anything to do with Blake's death, then Peter and the rest of our men obviously weren't killed by Al Hasan either. Yet someone knew about both missions, and they were ready for us." She drew in a breath and flexed her wrist. Jax could tell it was giving her trouble. "That suggests someone gave a heads-up we were coming . . . someone from the inside, as we believe."

Jax stopped. "The only question is who? Everyone who was under suspicion is dead, with the exception of you, and I know you didn't have anything to do with this." He paused for a moment. "I can't wrap my head around Coleman being behind the attacks either."

Sympathy showed in her eyes. "I know it's hard, but who else is there?" She winced when her wrist bumped against her body.

As much as he didn't want to believe Coleman was behind the betrayal, it was a huge coincidence that their rescue unit was ambushed, and he and Erin almost died because someone knew they were coming.

He shelved his doubts for the moment. "Let me have a look at that wrist," he told her and gently removed it from the sling. The way she was favoring it assured him it had gotten worse. After he unwrapped the wrist, he could see that the stress of their nonstop trek taking its toll.

"Where's the salve Basar gave you?" he asked, trying not to show her how worried he was.

"My backpack," she managed through gritted teeth.

Jax dug it out and applied a liberal amount to her wrist, then rewrapped it before easing it back into the sling.

Once finished, he glanced around, a sense of helplessness settling around him that he fought to control. "We still have a long way to go. We sure could use some help." With too many miles between them and the safe house, the stakes were high, and it was the two of them against a possibly huge army. "Can I see your burner phone?" he asked, and she took it out and handed it to him, a confused look on her face.

"I'm calling Al Hasan. Maybe he can assist." Desperate, Jax called the number, only to have it go straight to voicemail.

He frowned. "He's not answering." With no other option, they started walking again.

Jax was too exhausted to think clearly any longer. Putting one foot in front of the other was its own struggle. They'd covered several miles in silence when they crested a small knoll and spotted a dilapidated house a short distance ahead. Jax's footsteps froze. Seconds later Erin saw what he did. He motioned to the grove of trees close by, and they took cover.

Taking out his binoculars, he focused in on the house. "It doesn't appear to have been occupied for a while, so maybe we can take shelter there. Let's circle around to the side to be safe."

She nodded, and they slowly eased toward the house, keeping as close to the trees as possible. Once they reached the house, Jax edged toward the closest window and peered inside. He couldn't see any sign that the house had been occupied in a while.

"It's empty," he said, and she joined him at the front of the house. It took several tries before the rusted door finally opened. Jax drew his weapon and slipped inside. Erin did the same.

Erin tucked her weapon into her jacket and shrugged out of her backpack. There was a woodstove in the corner of the room. "Can we make a fire?" she wondered aloud. "It's so cold, even in here, and we're both frozen."

"We probably shouldn't, but we can't risk hypothermia either. We need to warm up." He gave her a gentle smile. "I'll go get some wood. You stay here and rest."

She didn't argue, appearing weary to the bone. She dropped to the floor without answering, and his concern for her well-being skyrocketed.

Keeping a careful eye on the surrounding countryside, Jax gathered wood as quickly as possible then carried it inside. Having a fire was risky. The smoke could give their position away.

Jax piled small twigs for kindling first, then wood into the stove, then lit the wood. The dampness of the wood, coupled with the lack of accelerant, had him wondering if it would catch. When it finally smoldered, Erin inched closer. As he watched her rub her chafed hands, he wondered if he would be able to keep her safe against the impossible situations they faced.

Jax sat next to her, dug in his backpack, and found a couple of power bars he'd stashed there. He handed her one, and she smiled her gratitude.

Sitting there, simply enjoying the fire and the food had him wondering what it would be like if he and Erin no longer faced the dangers they did right now. If it was just the two of them in some quiet mountain hideaway, enjoying the rest of their lives together. The thought gave him courage to keep fighting. He couldn't let the thugs who had done so much damage deprive them of the possibility of a future.

He turned to her, his thoughts going back to one time in particular before Blake's death. "You know Blake talked about leaving the CIA before his death," he said, and she turned to him, her eyes wide, searching his face.

"He did? I didn't know." She shook her head. "Why do you think he wanted to get out? Why did he want me to leave so badly?"

Jax shook his head. "Maybe he saw something like this happening. Maybe he was afraid the people who ended up killing him would come after you because of your relationship with him. The perps might think Blake told you something or gave you something incriminating. They can't afford to take any chances."

Erin drew in a breath. "I wish I'd known what he was going through. I could have helped him. Kept him safe. Convinced him to talk to someone. He might still be alive if I had."

Jax placed his hand over her good hand. "I feel the same way, but whatever Blake was involved in, I think he was trying to work it out himself. He was trying to protect us." As he looked into her eyes, his chest constricted. There was no way he was going to let Erin take the fall for criminal acts committed by some murderers. He'd find out who was behind the attacks, and he'd bring the people responsible to justice, even if it cost him his life.

Before he could manage a word, the burner phone rang. Jax's gaze flew to her, seeing her surprise.

He recognized the number right way. It was Al Hasan.

Chapter Thirteen

"Listen carefully," Al Hasan said in lieu of a greeting. The tension in his voice had Jax sitting up straighter, giving the call his full attention. "What is happening to you has nothing to do with weapons smuggling. It never did. It's far worse."

All color left his face. His expression froze in place. Jax put the phone on speaker so Erin could hear. "What do you mean it has nothing to do with weapons?"

"Because it doesn't. You've been led to believe you're fighting to keep weapons out of dangerous criminal hands, but what happened to your people has nothing to do with weapons."

"Then what does it have to do with?" Jax asked, his gaze locking on Erin's.

"Heroin." The word resounded, surprising them both.

"Drugs?" Erin whispered in shock. "I find that hard to believe."

"It's true," Al Hasan said. "This is about drugs. There never was a new terrorist threat or a training camp. It's about heroin, and plenty of it. Our people are drowning in it, destroying their lives with it."

"The men we captured gave up something," Jax deduced. "They told you who is behind this, didn't they?"

The silence that followed meant Al Hasan knew the answer.

"I cannot say," Al Hasan said at last. "That is for you to figure out, but you should know your enemies go much higher up the command chain than you think."

Jax's gaze pierced hers. "Like, how high? You know something more than you're saying, and we need your help. We're out here all alone, and we're outnumbered. I'm asking you to tell us what you have."

"I cannot tell you what I don't know," Al Hasan insisted. "But for an operation to be as successful as this one has been for so long, it takes a lot of power and money to grease the wheels."

As much as she wished differently, Al Hasan wasn't going to give them anything more.

"Your own people are trying to kill you, and they won't stop until you're both dead. You can't go back to the States. They'll find another way to eliminate the problem you pose. I suggest you find a way to disappear." Al Hasan didn't mince words, and fear pooled inside her.

Where could they possibly go to escape? "How many men are there?" she asked, her thoughts churning.

"Dozens. They are led by your people, along with some Afghan traitors, like the ones we killed. They have no allegiance. Their loyalty is to whoever pays them the most money."

Erin drew in an unsteady breath. "That's why we need your help. We'll never get out of the country alone on our own, and we can't trust our people."

The length of time it took Al Hasan to answer did little to ease Erin's fears.

"Where are you now?" he asked.

Jax covered the speaker. "I don't think we have a choice. We need his help. It may be our only way out."

Erin wanted to believe him, but she couldn't let go of her doubts. She grabbed his arm. "Do you think we can trust our lives to him?" What if everything Al Hasan had done so far was to gain their trust, then trap them?

Jax held her gaze, his answer less than reassuring. "No, but right now he's all we've got."

While they continued to peer into each other's eyes, Erin finally gave in with a weighty sigh. "You're right. Do it."

She prayed that they hadn't just sealed their deaths by giving their location to the one person the CIA had led them to believe was a weapons dealer as well as a terrorist.

Jax gave Al Hasan their coordinates.

"Good, I can help you. I'll get back to you within the hour with a plan. In the meantime, keep out of sight. And keep moving." With those somber words still ringing in the air between them, the call ended.

Jax's blew out a breath. "He's right. We have to keep going. Once we reach the city, we should be able to blend in easy enough. It's something, I guess." He looked at her without much confidence before rising and holding out his hand to her.

Erin let him pull her to her feet, then grabbed her backpack and shouldered it while Jax did the same. He went outside and brought in a pile of snow, tossing it on the burning fire. It took several trips to extinguish the flames in the stove. Once they were finished, he turned to her, exhaustion clinging to every line on his face. "Ready?" he asked.

She stood up taller and forced a smile for his sake. "I'm ready."

They headed out into the twilight of another fading day.

"We'll be traveling at night. It won't be easy," Jax said, his tone discouraging.

She touched his arm. "I know this is hard, but we have to keep going. We can't let them win, Jax. We have to find a way back to the States to retrieve the evidence Blake left for us. And when we do, we can bring those people down and make them pay for what they've done to Blake and the rest of our friends."

He smiled and scraped back a loose strand of her hair from her face. "You're right, they've done enormous damage already. They have to be stopped." He leaned close and touched his lips to her forehead before letting her go.

The bitter cold seeped into her bones, making the thick jacket she wore seem like nothing at all. They couldn't stop. Their own people were hunting them, determined to lay the blame for everything on Jax and Erin before they killed them. And all because of greed. All the innocent lives lost, all the pain and suffering, had been to keep their drug smuggling operation secret. Whoever was behind this was ruthless. She and Jax were mere pawns in their game.

She shuddered at how hopeless their situation seemed. They had lost too much already. Blake, no matter what he'd done wrong, would always be her friend. He didn't deserve to die the way he did because of drugs.

Now Jax's life was on the line, and she was terrified they wouldn't make it out of Pakistan alive. With her heart breaking and helplessness threatening to drown her, Erin silently prayed for God's protection. *We need You, Lord. We can't do this by ourselves. There are too many of them and only two of us. I'm unclear who is behind this plot. Please, show us the way out of here. Please don't let us die here in vain.*

When her prayer ended, she waited for some sign. Some sense of guidance. As she listened to the sounds of the night settling around them, Erin realized her answer was standing right in front of her. Jax. He was her answer. God had put him in her life, shown her that it was possible for her to find happiness beyond the Agency, and to leave this shadow life behind for good. He wasn't going to let them die out here. Not like this. Together, with God's help, they'd weather this storm, and when it was over, they'd set their own course in life—whether together or apart.

* * *

Your own people are trying to kill you. . . . Jax couldn't get Al Hasan's words out of his head. Members of the same team as he and Erin—people sworn to protect their country at all cost—were trying to destroy them to flood the country with drugs that would damage thousands of lives. He couldn't make it add up in his head.

They'd all taken the oath to protect the US with their lives. How was it possible? He thought about the ambush at the abandoned airstrip. How had those men known of the location? There was only one plausible explanation, but his gut wouldn't let him accept it. Coleman was a war hero and larger than life. Jax had read about his heroic efforts to free a village from Taliban control. How could someone like that go from being a hero to a drug smuggler?

The exhaustion weighing his limbs down made thinking clearly next to impossible. He and Erin had been walking for hours without a break. Even though it was the middle of the night, they'd skirted around several small villages to keep from calling undue attention to themselves. But they were both working on fumes alone. They couldn't go much further.

"Let's stop to rest," Jax said and looked for a good place to sit for a while. He found a downed tree trunk and took off his backpack. Erin did the same. She grabbed her bottle of water and gulped some down.

He was too exhausted to do more than sit. "We can't keep going like this. Peshawar's still a long way off. Without rest and a proper meal, we'll never make it."

She handed him her water. "You're right. This cold isn't helping. We need shelter and food." Erin pulled out the map again and clicked on her flashlight.

Jax scanned the map. If he remembered correctly, misdirected drone strikes on this side of the border had taken out a couple of villages a few years back. It had been a point of contention between the US and Pakistani governments for some time afterwards. Jax found the spot and pointed it out.

"Here. There are a couple of villages that suffered heavy bombing. If we can make it to one of them, maybe we can find a deserted place to hole up for a while. Perhaps find some food even."

The closest spot was a good five miles away. He hoped they were making the right decision because by taking this route, they'd be adding more miles to their journey and they were already exhausted.

"We should be there by daybreak," she said and managed a semi-smile. "It's worth a shot."

Erin extinguished her flashlight, but Jax didn't move. "Let's rest for a little while longer," he told her, then studied her silhouette in the darkness. "How's your wrist?"

"Better. The salve really works, despite the strain of the hike." She flexed her wrist for him to see. "I think I can lose the sling for now."

As glad as he was that she was feeling better, he surmised that they were going to need all their strength and wits to survive this journey.

"Do you think it's possible that Coleman has gone rogue?" she asked, her question mirroring his previous thoughts.

Jax shrugged, his heart weary. "I don't want to believe it, but we can't take the chance of contacting him after what happened the last time, which means we're on our own for now." Jax strapped on his backpack and gathered his waning strength. They had to keep pushing forward if they were going to reach the village by first light.

With a bone-weary sigh, Erin clambered to her feet then shouldered her backpack.

He wished he could reassure her that everything was going to be okay, but from where they stood right now, nothing could be further from the truth.

As they headed for the first abandoned village, an unsettling thought niggled at his brain. The attack on the Afghan ambassador didn't make sense. If Coleman was behind the attacks and he was smuggling heroin out of Afghanistan, why would he attack his friend, and possibly his business partner? Unless . . .

He shared his fears with Erin.

"You think it's possible that the ambassador is connected to all of this?" She stopped walking, sucking in a breath. "What if he's the one responsible for getting the heroin into the US?"

Jax peered into her eyes, shock plastered on his face. "He and Coleman have been friends for years. If Coleman is responsible for this, it makes sense."

"Maybe Coleman was working with the ambassador and something went wrong in the relationship. Perhaps the ambassador threatened to turn Coleman in and . . ." she left the rest unsaid, but he knew what she meant. Coleman tried to kill the ambassador and may have succeeded. If this were true, then Coleman was covering up his crimes. Tying up loose ends. And they were the next loose ones on his list. He couldn't allow them to live.

Chapter Fourteen

Her legs felt like rubber. She wasn't sure how much farther she could go. They were both working on next to zero sleep. Lack of proper food and fear was affecting her rational thinking.

The woods they'd been traveling through had begun to thin as daylight drew near.

"We should be getting close," Jax said. "Let's take another look at the map."

Erin dug it out of her backpack, and he flicked on the light. "We're almost there. According to the map, we should be right on top of the village."

Nodding, he eased ahead while Erin followed close behind. The trees cleared away. Shadows still covered most of the land, making it impossible to see anything. Jax took out his binoculars and switched them onto night vision capability. "There it is." He pointed straight ahead, handing her the binoculars.

Erin zeroed in on the location. The village lay inactive, like a pile of debris. Nothing stirred, not even an animal.

"It doesn't look as if it's ever been rebuilt," she told him, a little doubtful. "I sure hope it's safe there."

He drew in a breath and gripped her hand. "Lord, we're asking for Your protection," he prayed and then stepped out into the open, drawing his weapon.

Erin did the same, fear slithering down her spine as she scanned the filmy darkness, expecting trouble. What if the men coming after them had anticipated their next move and were waiting for them in the village? If it were true and they were being chased by fellow CIA agents, they wouldn't stand a chance.

Before they reached the first building, Jax stopped and waited for her to draw near. "Let's stay as close to the edge of the buildings as possible," he whispered. "We don't know what to expect. They could have snipers set up."

The reminder of what might be waiting for them had her on full alert.

Jax headed forward with Erin glued to his side. Even in the semi-darkness they'd be moving targets to anyone using night vision.

At the edge of the building, Jax surveyed the area, uncertainty written on his face. "So far so good. I don't see anyone. Let's go inside and search the place."

She nodded, and they eased inside. The four walls held nothing but rubble. Not exactly ideal for shelter.

"It doesn't look as if it's inhabited. No doubt, the villagers moved on to some place safer. Let's see if we can find a better spot to take cover," Jax said.

A half dozen buildings littered the area, most in the same state as the one they'd entered. "We'll have better luck if we split up," Erin said. She could tell he didn't like the idea, but they needed to search the village quickly to determine if it were safe.

He finally gave in. "All right, but keep your eyes open and get out of there if anything looks hinky. The people coming after us might not be here, but we don't know if the place is deserted."

As daylight continued to break, Erin pointed to the opposite side of the street running through the village. "I'll start over there. If anything comes up, yell."

She hurried across the road, her heartbeat drowning out most sounds. The hair on the back of her neck stood at full attention. They were being watched, she could feel it.

The first building she came to had standing walls and a roof. At least it was something. Inside, it appeared to have once been a living quarters. The damage sustained wasn't nearly as extensive as the previous building. She glanced around, her weapon drawn, an eerie feeling of being spied upon pervading her senses.

Struggling to keep paranoia at bay, she searched the few rooms of the place. There was a stove they could use to keep warm. The owner of the place had left little else behind. A few bowls in what served as the kitchen. A couple of pillows in the living area. No food.

Two more buildings were on the same side. Keeping her weapon at the ready, Erin made her way to the next one, slightly bigger and appearing to be some type of business. She was almost inside the door when a shot ricocheted inches from her head. She ducked as another shot pinged, equally close enough to leave its ringing in her ears. The flash came from the building on Jax's side.

"Erin, are you okay?" He called out, unable to disguise the fear in his tone.

"I'm okay, but there's a shooter on your side, one building over."

"Stay where you are." He skirted the wall then disappeared into the building.

She didn't obey. He could be walking into an ambush, and she had to have his back.

Firing off several rounds to put the shooter in retreat, Erin sprinted across the street, pasted herself against the walk, then slipped inside.

Jax was nowhere in sight. Her pulse went crazy, making normal breathing an impossible task. She searched the first room. Nothing, but there were obvious signs someone had been living there. Shoes close to the door. Mismatched furniture formed a makeshift living space. Clothing was strewn over the dirt floor.

She was ready to move on to the next room when the sound of scuffling reached her ears. She ran toward the sound.

Jax and another man wrestled on the dirt floor. Erin charged for them, her weapon aimed at the man fighting with Jax.

"Get your hands in the air," she ordered. The man broke free and pushed past her. She grabbed him by the collar before he could get away. "Oh no, you don't," she said and shoved him against the wall. With her weapon pointed at his head, Jax yanked the man around. Once she caught a good look at him, she couldn't believe what she was seeing. It was a boy, barely a teenager.

Erin glanced at Jax's surprised face. "Who are you?" she asked the boy, whose huge, fearful brown eyes darted between her and Jax.

He seemed incapable of speaking.

Erin let the boy go. "What's your name," she asked in a gentler tone.

"My name . . . Dawoud." he stammered.

"What are you doing here, Dawoud, and where did you get that weapon?" Jax pointed at the gun.

The boy's eyes were as large as globes. "I live . . . here," he said in a whisper. "This is my home."

Erin stared at the boy, trying to decide if he was telling the truth. "Where are your parents . . . mother, father?"

Dawoud swallowed, his gaze dropping. "They dead. Airstrike. All my people . . . killed. Everyone in the village." Tears brimmed his eyes as he spoke of his family. Erin couldn't imagine how difficult it was to lose his entire family and be left alone to survive.

"Why were you shooting at us?" she asked, pointing at his weapon.

Dawoud's eyes shot to hers. He shrugged. "I think you were . . . them. I . . . afraid."

Jax's gaze sliced to Erin. "Them?" he repeated.

"Drug runners. They . . . store drugs here. They left gun. I take." Dawoud insisted, shaking his head.

Shocked, Erin couldn't believe what the boy said. Dawoud confirmed what Al Hasan told them. "How old are you?" she asked. He didn't appear old enough to be a teen, much less someone who could live on his own.

"Me fourteen," the boy said defensively, his chin jutting up.

"And you live here?" She pointed at the boy, then at the ground. "How long?" She wanted to believe him, but they couldn't afford to take unnecessary risks.

"Four . . . how you say . . . years since airstrike." He pointed at the ground. "I stay here . . . all alone," he said proudly.

"How did you learn to speak English?" Erin asked.

"Before airstrike . . . I watched CNN. After village destroyed, I listened to the men."

Erin swiveled to Jax and motioned outside. Then she whirled and held up the palm of her hand in Dawoud's direction. "Stay here and don't try leaving. We'll be right back."

Jax followed her outside. Once they were out of earshot, he asked. "Do you believe him?"

Of all the things they'd fought their way through, all the lies they'd been fed, Dawoud was the first person they'd run across recently that she truly did believe.

* * *

"I do. I think he's telling the truth, and he may be able to shed some light on the people moving the drugs through here."

Jax glanced back over his shoulder. He thought the same thing. "Poor kid. I can't imagine what he's been through, losing his entire family like that. Living in fear for years."

Erin touched his arm. "Me neither. I want to find a way to help him. He deserves a chance at a normal life, and this isn't it."

Jax squeezed her hand and turned back to the door. "Let's go see what he knows."

Together, they went back inside. Dawoud sat on the floor close to the same spot where they'd left him. When they came into the room, his head shot up, fear in his eyes. He appeared ready to bolt.

"Relax, son, we're not going to hurt you," Jax assured him and knelt in front of the boy. "But we need you to tell us everything you know about these men who routed drugs through here." When he saw the boy didn't understand, he said, "Men . . . drugs . . . where? Who?"

Dawoud's eyebrows formed a vee. "Why trust you? I trust drug men, then they try to kill me."

Jax leaned back on his haunches, unable to hide the shock. "Those men tried to kill you? Why?"

He lifted his shoulders. "Men angry. No trust me. Treat me like . . . how you say . . . slave. They shoot me here." He pointed to his right side.

Jax couldn't believe what he'd heard. "How'd you get treatment for the shot?" When it became clear Dawoud didn't understand Jax said, "Doctor? Hospital?"

Dawoud shook his head and pointed to his chest. "Me the doctor." He acted out pulling the bullet out with his fingers then lifted his shirt to show them the wound.

Jax took a closer look. "You did a good job, Dawoud."

The boy beamed.

"Can you tell us what those men looked like?" Erin asked, kneeling next to Jax. She pointed at her face and repeated the word *men*.

Dawoud hesitated then held up two fingers. "Two Americans. Others Afghan."

Jax pressed for answers because time was running out for them and for Dawoud. "Can you tell us exactly what the two Americans looked like?" He pointed at his face and repeated the word "Americans."

Dawoud shook his head, distrust in his eyes. "Don't know. Covered faces."

"Then how did you know they were Americans?" Erin asked, baffled by his answer.

"They talk American, like you."

Jax's head whipped around so that he could see Erin's reaction. She was just as surprised as he was. "When was the last time the men were here?" Jax asked. He felt bad for the boy, all alone and barely surviving. He repeated the words "last time."

Dawoud thought about the question for a moment. He searched through the rubble on the floor and found a calendar written in Pashto. He pointed at a specific day and said, "Today." Then he flipped through the pages and pointed at different periods of time. From that, Jax gleaned that the drug runners showed up every few months and the last time they'd been there was over a month ago.

Which meant the men could return at any time.

"Dawoud, we need to get you out of here. It's not safe for you to stay here any longer. If those men come back, they might try to finish the job." Then he reduced what he'd said to a single word, "danger," then added, "you must leave."

Dawoud shook his head vigorously. "No, This my home. They come, I hide in woods. No leave."

"How do you stay warm? It's freezing in here," Jax glanced around the room. There was no stove in sight. He demonstrated rubbing one's arms to get warm.

The boy got to his feet and disappeared into another room. Exchanging a look, Erin and Jax followed. In what appeared to be a bedroom, on the dirt floor, a pile of wood burned. Dawoud sat down next to the fire and added some additional sticks from a pile close by.

Erin went over to the fire and warmed her hands. "No family?" she asked.

Dawoud shook his head. "No. My mother's family in Peshawar. I not see them."

"Maybe we can help you find them?" Erin said, but Dawoud didn't appear open to the idea.

"How are you surviving here on your own? What do you eat?" Jax asked when the boy refused to make eye contact. Jax demonstrated eating with his hands.

Dawoud glanced up. "I hunt. Wild goat." His fingers flailed on his head, describing an animal with antlers.

Jax smiled at the boy's passion. "You wouldn't happen to have some of that goat meat lying around that you could share with us, would you?"

Dawoud hopped to his feet, his brooding mood lifting. "Yes." Once the boy was gone, Jax went to where Erin stood.

"The poor kid. If they find him here again, they'll kill him," she said. He could read her thoughts. She wanted to help Dawoud find his mother's family.

"We can't force him to come with us," Jax said and had a thought. "But if we can get the name of his relatives near Peshawar and see if we can have someone look them up once we're safe. Maybe they can rescue the boy."

She faced him, her eyes shining with tears. He drew her into his arms and held her close. He loved her so much. Wanted her to feel the same way about him. At times, he believed she did. At others, he wasn't so sure.

If this mission had taught him anything, it was that this was his final one. He'd lost too many good men to this war. Blake. Peter. Sam, Dylan, Tyler. Kabir. The names were mounting. So many gone before their time. It wasn't worth it to him any longer. And he'd do his best to convince Erin to get out before it cost her life as well.

She touched his face tenderly, a smile playing on her lips. "We're going to get through this, Jax. I know we are. We have to trust God to bring us home safely."

He clasped her hand in his. He so wanted to believe her, but it felt as if they'd been fighting alone for so long, and they still had no real idea how they were going to get back to the States. And even if they did, he didn't know if the information Blake left in the safety deposit box was still there. Without it, how would they ever clear Erin's name?

As he continued to watch her, the strength he saw in her had him relinquishing his own fears. She was right. God hadn't brought them all this way to let them down. He needed his faith to be stronger than his fears.

Chapter Fifteen

"Someone's coming!" Dawoud shook her arm hard. Erin's eyes flew open. She stared into dark eyes filled with real terror. "We leave. They kill us."

Erin jumped to her feet, aware of Jax getting up.

"How many?" she asked the boy.

"Don't know. Five? Six?"

"How close are they?" Erin asked, grabbing her backpack while Jax extinguished the fire.

"Very close to village." Dawoud was shaking.

"We have to get going. If they find us, we'll all be dead," Jax said. "Show us the best place to hide."

They followed the boy out of the house. He pointed to the left. "They are coming from there," he whispered.

"Then we need to head in the opposite way," Erin said then headed right toward the trees one hundred feet away, her breath chilling in the night air.

When they reached the last building, Erin flattened herself against it and peeked around the side. She didn't see anyone. Time was critical. The men were coming through the woods fast.

Jax took the lead. She and Dawoud followed him out into the open. Just a few more steps. They were almost at the forest's edge.

"I see them," someone yelled.

Her legs threatened to buckle. They'd been spotted.

"Run," Jax yelled, and they scrambled for the trees.

By the time they reached the first set of trees, bullets rained down on them from multiple weapons.

Erin dove for the tree coverage with Jax and Dawoud close behind.

"We're outmanned, and we can't fight them. We have to escape," Erin said as they charged through the forest shoving branches aside as they ran. Her breath burned in her lungs.

Dawoud was agile and fast. He passed her easily. Jax caught up with her quickly. "We can't outrun them, and we can't fight them off." The desperation in his voice was hard to take.

"Don't give up on us, Jax. We have to keep fighting."

She'd barely spoken the words when the gunshots fired in their directions were met with return fire.

Erin stopped abruptly. "Wait, is that . . . ?"

Relief flooded Jax's expression and he grinned. "It is. The only question is who?"

"Let's find out." She glanced around looking for Dawoud. "Where did he go?"

"He's probably still running. The boy certainly knows how to look out for himself. Let's see if we can give assistance to the people who are helping us, then we'll go back and find him."

With Jax close, they eased back through the trees. From where they stood, it appeared the entire town was ablaze with gunfire. The people pursuing them had now retreated far into the woods. Dozens of armed men advanced on them.

Shock rippled through her when Erin spotted someone familiar. "That's Al Hasan." She pointed to the leader whom they'd once believed to be a terrorist. He was there to save their lives. Again. Maybe it was the fact he'd been framed by the same people that made him sympathetic to their plight.

As the men continued firing as they retreated, Al Hasan's troops soon gained the upper hand.

Erin and Jax left their spot and inched toward the firefight. They'd taken only a few steps when the shooting suddenly stopped, followed by an eerie silence.

Her gaze shot to Jax as they entered the forest where the shots had come from. Right away, they were met with armed soldiers.

"Drop your weapons." Erin recognized the speaker as one of Al Hasan's men.

"Leave them be. They are friends," Al Hasan ordered, coming to where they stood. "So, I saved your lives again," he said without expression, yet Erin believed he was teasing.

Erin smiled. She was never so happy to see anyone in her life. "You did, and we're grateful." She watched Jax extend his hand toward Al Hasan. Once Al Hasan shook hands with him, he glanced over his shoulder. "I'm sorry to say the men who were following you are all dead."

Shocked, Erin couldn't believe it. "All of them?"

Al Hasan nodded. "There were six in total, but they aren't the only ones tracking you."

Her heart sank. This wasn't the news she wanted to hear.

"My men checked. They are all Afghans. Mercenaries for hire, paid by your people, no doubt. The others are still out there somewhere. They'll keep coming. It's not safe for you here. You have to leave immediately."

She and Jax were both dead tired and running out of options. She'd managed to get a couple of hours' sleep. It would have to do. The safe house in Peshawar was no longer an option. If Coleman was the one who ordered their deaths, he'd anticipate their next move and have men waiting for them there.

"I still can't believe this is all because of heroin," Erin said.

Al Hasan's stone expression didn't change. "I now believe it's more than just the heroin. The money made from the drugs can buy a lot of weapons. The heroin is a means of funding other far more malicious activities, and the people behind this do not care about the consequences. The drugs hit the streets of your country, where they bring premium prices. The money is then funneled back to our country to buy weapons for men who are determined to keep our country in turmoil for their own gain."

And the deadly cycle continued year after year. Erin could understand why Al Hasan and others like him were fed up with the ramifications that resulted from a few men's greed. They wanted their country back without the interference of thugs.

"I have a friend who lives outside Peshawar. He can help you arrange passage out of Pakistan." Al Hasan gave them his friend's name and cell number. "I'll call him and tell him to watch you. You have to be careful, though. There are . . . many dangerous people in that part of the country. Allegiances lie with some of the worst terrorists around. Some who would take pleasure in handing you over to the enemy for the right price."

Erin shivered as she thought about what lay ahead. The walls were closing in around them and she had no idea where to turn for safe harbor. She prayed Al Hasan's friend was trustworthy.

"I have supplies that will help make the journey easier." Al Hasan snapped his fingers and one of his men came forward carrying a backpack. Al Hasan handed it to Jax. "There is food and water. Medical supplies. Extra weapons and ammunition. You have a long road ahead of you, and, as you can see, it won't be easy."

Jax nodded their gratitude. "Thank you."

Movement behind them had Erin whirling around. Dawoud slowly emerged and joined them.

Al Hasan had proven himself more than resourceful. Perhaps he could help locate the boy's family. She said, "This is Dawoud. He lost his family to the airstrikes that destroyed his village a few years back. I wonder if you can help him out. Dawoud has family near Peshawar. His mother's people."

Al Hasan stared at the boy for the longest time, his expression deadpan as always. "I can help. I know people in Peshawar. I'll ask around. In the meantime, he'll be under my protection," he assured them.

Although she and Jax had a long way to go before they could find peace, at least she wouldn't have to worry about Dawoud's safety.

Erin faced the boy again, his fear easy to see. She wanted to put his mind at ease. She smiled at him. "You'll be safe now. You can trust this man. He'll protect you and help you find your family."

Dawoud wasn't convinced, but he managed a weak nod. Erin couldn't imagine the horrific things he'd witnessed at such a young age. He'd lost his ability to trust. To be a kid. Maybe with Al Hasan's help, he could get trust back.

Jax came over and clasped Dawoud's shoulder, smiling down at the boy. "Take care of yourself, Dawoud. Let Al Hasan help you find your family." He glanced back at the deserted village. "This is no way for you to live."

With tears in his eyes, Dawoud took Jax by surprise and hugged him close. Erin witnessed the wealth of emotions in Jax's eyes as he held the boy tight a moment longer before letting him go.

Erin nodded to Al Hasan while Jax shook his hand. With a final look at Dawoud, they headed away from the village. She prayed that Dawoud would find his mother's family and he would find a happy ending in the future. For her and Jax, the future was something they couldn't afford to hope for yet. Too much was at stake. Their own people were coming after them, and the only person they'd found trustworthy so far besides a young boy was the CIA's most wanted terrorist.

* * *

Jax stared at the map once more. "It's best if we keep as far away from Peshawar as we can. If we stay to the east, there should be enough tree coverage to conceal us from anyone on the lookout."

They'd put several miles between themselves and Al Hasan and his men before taking a much-needed break.

Erin barely glanced at the map. "I hope we can trust Al Hasan's friend. After everything we've been through, trust is something that doesn't come easy anymore."

She obviously had her doubts. He did too. "So far, Al Hasan is the only one I do trust. Hopefully, that will prove true of his friend as well."

With a hint of a nod, Erin folded the map and put it away before looking around. "I still can't fathom Coleman being behind all of this. He's a hero. How could someone like that become involved in smuggling drugs? Murder?"

Jax had been struggling to reconcile the hero he looked up to with someone capable of killing his own people for money. "I guess everyone has their price, and when you're threatened, who knows what any of us are capable of doing." Still, the thought of Coleman arranging the deaths of his own agents sickened Jax.

He studied Erin. She was barely hanging on, as was he, and he wasn't sure how much farther either of them could go. He hoped Al Hasan's friend proved helpful.

One of his favorite verses from the Bible popped into his head. *I can do all things through Christ which strengtheneth me.* A message sent to his heart from God. On their own, they could do nothing, but with God, all things were possible. They'd get through this by trusting Him.

Jax clasped her shoulder, and she turned to look at him. Weariness marred her beauty. "We're going to be okay," he whispered with a faint smile, their gazes tangling.

She wanted to believe him, he could see. "I hope you're right, because I can't see a good ending to all of this."

Jax pulled her into his embrace and held her close, his chin resting on her head.

"Right now, you're all that I believe in besides God," she murmured, and his heart soared.

"Then believe me when I tell you we're going to make it through. We're not going to let them win. We've lost too many good people to let them win this time."

She nodded against his chest, still holding him tight. "I can't believe they're all gone. And Peter—he has a family!" She jerked her head to peer into his eyes. "Two young kids. How are we going to tell Sarah that her husband is dead?"

Jax had no answer. If Coleman was truly behind this, then he'd already begun to spin the story to frame them. Jax didn't want to voice his concerns aloud. He didn't want Erin to stop fighting. "We'd better keep moving," he said instead. "If Al Hasan is correct, we don't have much breathing room."

Erin hugged him tightly then let him go, staring up into his eyes. "You're right." She shook her head. "I'll be so glad when this is over."

He managed a smile because he couldn't tell her his darkest thoughts. The bad outcome she'd mentioned churned in his stomach.

As they continued to watch each other, she drew in a breath, her eyes growing large. He knew he was giving away all sorts of things. His heart was hers to take. He loved her and he was certain about where he wanted their future to go, if God blessed them with a second chance to have one. It was up to her to figure what she wanted.

He framed her face. Saw the uncertainty in her eyes, then leaned down and gently kissed her with everything he felt inside reflected in his touch.

With a strangled whimper, Erin ended the kiss and clung to him. He wrapped her in his arms and held her close. Just for a second, the world with its troubles faded away and it was the two of them, and he was so in love with her. She sighed deeply, then let him go, touching his cheek briefly. "We'd better go, it'll be dark soon. It would be nice to reach Al Hasan's friend before nightfall."

She was right. Traveling at night into unknown territory was dangerous. Al Hasan had warned them about the area being unstable. Would they be walking into a whole different set of bad men before they had the chance to figure out what was really going on?

Chapter Sixteen

They crested a hill as twilight settled in. The city lights of Peshawar spread out before them. Somewhere inside the city was a CIA safe house, yet they didn't dare go there for protection.

"Al Hasan said his friend lives east of the city," Jax said.

They slowly descended the hill. Erin's heart thundered against her chest. Al Hasan said his friend could get them safe passage out of Pakistan. If they could get to Punjab, and from there make it into India, they could reach out to some of their contacts and hopefully make it into the US undetected. It was a longshot, but, right now, the only one they had.

The village of Lowhadu was tucked between the bustling metropolis of Peshawar and the distant city of Kohat. As they headed toward the small town, every step she made had her jumping at the noise.

Despite the modern city close by, Lowhadu was still caught in the past. Somewhere in the distance, a dog barked. They stopped briefly to gain their bearings.

"Al Hasan said that his friend's place is off by itself at the far end of the village," Jax reminded her.

She drew in a fear-fueled breath, the hair on the back of her neck standing at full attention, not liking what she saw. It felt as if they were walking into yet another trap.

"Something feels off," she said, glancing Jax's way. The muscle working in his jaw proved he felt the same way.

"Let's circle around behind to get to his house. That way we can stay hidden from sight."

They eased around to the back of the village, weapons drawn. Erin found herself whirling at every little sound. Lights were on around town. Voices carried from nearby houses. Sheep bleated. Somewhere nearby another dog bayed.

Jax took out the burner phone and dialed their contact's number. "There's no answer," he said, ending the call.

Where was Al Hasan's friend? Why wasn't he responding to their call?

"This looks like the place," Jax said, pointing to the last house off by itself. "I'll go inside and check it out. Keep watch. You're right. Something about this doesn't feel right."

He barely got the words out when the burner phone in his pocket beeped. They hurried away from the house, hoping not to call undue attention to themselves. Jax pulled out the phone. "It's a text from Al Hasan." He quickly read the message. "We have to leave. His friend contacted him. They know we're coming here, Erin. It's another setup."

Erin turned and took off running from the village to the wilderness close by. Jax caught up with her easily enough. As they continued maneuvering through the thicket, her breath burned in her chest, yet she couldn't stop. The men tracking them knew they were here. How?

Once they'd put distance between themselves and the village, Jax stopped abruptly. She did the same, her gaze darting around the area, thoughts scattered. The enemy was always one step ahead of them.

With the phone still in his hand, Jax called Al Hasan. "What's going on? Where's your friend, and how did they know where to find us?" Anger mixed with accusation in his tone. She couldn't blame him. Al Hasan was the only person who knew where they were going. Even though he had saved their lives multiple times, someone had alerted the enemy where to find them.

Jax listened to Al Hasan's answer, his gaze latched onto Erin. "All right, what's our best escape route from here?" After a minute, Jax said, "Okay, thanks." He ended the call and shoved the phone back into his pocket.

"Al Hasan got a call from his friend a little before we arrived. He said that his friend spotted several Americans wandering around the village earlier in the day and he got nervous. He left for Kohat. When he arrived, he alerted Al Hasan to what was happening. According to Al Hasan, if we can make it to Kohat, his friend can still get us out."

They couldn't go back the way they'd come. Peshawar was too risky. Kohat was another thirty miles away, and the people coming after them were closer than she liked.

"We'll have to do our best to stay out of sight," Jax said, reading her thoughts. "The darkness will help, but they're obviously looking for us."

"If they were here earlier, where are they now?" Erin asked.

"I don't know. Maybe when they didn't find us, they moved on to Peshawar. If they're CIA, then they'll know about the safe house. They'll be expecting us to head that way. Hopefully, they won't think to look in Kohat."

Erin blew out a frustrated sigh. "You're right, they would expect us to be heading for the safe house." She remembered something she'd read about in the past. "Didn't the army seize a huge cache of weapons near Kohat last year?"

His gaze whipped to hers. "That's right. Several dozen weapons as well as more than seven thousand rounds of various caliber ammo was recovered in that raid. . . . You think the weapons are the ones being funneled into Afghanistan through Kohat and the Mendiu Pass?"

"I think it's likely, assuming Coleman is the one in charge of the operation, and he's recruited agents to help him with the transport. Blake being one of them . . ." she stopped as a chilling thought occurred. "Do you think some of the others might have been involved?" She thought about her teammates. Dylan. Sam. Tyler. She couldn't imagine them capable of such treachery, yet she hadn't thought Blake capable either.

"I don't want to think so, but until we know how far this goes, we can't reject the idea," Jax said.

"But why take them all out? If they were involved, why would Coleman kill them all?" It didn't make sense. She went back to her original thought. "If Coleman is in charge and he coordinates the smuggling of the heroin out of Afghanistan, presumably with the help of the ambassador through the embassy's plane, once the drugs hit the US, they would have to have dealers they relied on to move the product. Then, once the money is collected, they'd buy the weapons on the black market and funnel them back into Afghanistan to fund who knows what acts of terror. It's a foolproof operation. So why kill Blake? The others?"

Jax considered her question. "Obviously, Blake was having second thoughts. Regretting his involvement. He might have threatened to blow the operation wide open, so Coleman had him killed."

Erin swallowed back her revulsion. "How large is this operation? To pull off something like this, and to keep it secret for so long, you have to have a lot of people involved at different levels of leadership, both here and in our country." She stopped as a disturbing thought occurred.
Do you think they know Blake was collecting evidence against them? Is that why they're so determined to kill us?"

Jax's gaze locked with hers. "I'd say it's a good possibility. I just hope they don't know about the safety deposit box yet. If they do, the evidence may already be gone."

The thought was chilling. If Coleman and his friend at the embassy had been running drugs for a while, perhaps even back when Coleman was still in the field, then they could have dozens of men involved along every step of the way. Even here in this area. Every second they were out in the open, they risked being spotted by someone working for Coleman. Each step of the way they'd be walking a tightrope, trying to stay alive long enough to clear their names—running from their own people, who were determined to stop the threat they posed.

* * *

Jax tried to recall what he knew about the region surrounding Kohat. Mountains and foothills dominated the area. The town itself was centered around a British-era fort, various bazaars, and a military cantonment.

The endless walking through rugged terrain burned his already-strained muscles. With too many miles ahead of them, and far too many unanswered questions rattling around in his head, Jax needed a break. "Mind if we stop for a second?" he asked, and she immediately shook her head.

"Not at all. I could use a break as well. My legs feel as if they're ready to give out underneath me." She took off her backpack and used it as a seat. He did the same.

Jax clicked on his flashlight and opened the backpack Al Hasan had given them. He took out two Afghan *bolanis*, their version of vegetable-stuffed flatbread, along with some grapes.

He handed one to Erin who took a bite, then closed her eyes. "This is delicious." She pointed to the spinach and cilantro filled flatbread. "Of course, Dawoud's goat was pretty good as well, especially for someone living off power bars and water."

He chuckled at what she said. "You're right. When we get back to the States, if I see another power bar, I think I might lose it." He dug into the bolani with vigor, savoring the flavors.

Erin joined in the laughter. "That's one of the many things I plan to give up." She stopped talking and he realized there was more to what she was saying.

He finished chewing. "What do you mean?" With his heart pounding, he had to know.

She wiped a crumb from her mouth, then faced him. "I want out, Jax. I don't think I have it in me to do this anymore. I'm leaving the CIA for good."

The hopelessness in her eyes tore at his heart. He clasped her hand. "Are you sure?" Part of him was elated that she wouldn't be in the line of fire any longer. The other part wondered where that left them.

She squeezed his hand and nodded. "I am. I'm going to take Blake's advice and get out. It's time, and I think he knew it." She stopped for a second. "I wished he'd taken his own advice and gotten out before he became involved in whatever ended up getting him killed."

Jax swallowed visibly. "Me too. I miss him. I don't care what he was part of, he's still my friend, and he didn't deserve what happened to him."

She smiled. "He didn't. None of them did." She finished the last of her bolani and wiped her hands.

"Do you have any idea what you'll want to do once you leave?" he asked because he needed answers. Would she choose him? If not, would he ever see her again?

She stared into space. "I have no idea," she said as if she hadn't contemplated the idea before. "Something plain vanilla, for sure."

He understood what she meant. Doing something mundane after the things they'd witnessed would be a welcomed relief.

"Maybe I'll work at a bank." She laughed as she thought about it. "Or maybe I'll write a book. I certainly have some interesting stories to tell."

He took her hand, brought it to his lips, and kissed it. "You'd make a good writer."

In the moonlight, he saw Erin swallow, her reaction to his touch there for him to see. She leaned close. He did the same. There were tears in her eyes, and he wondered why. He wanted to know. But he wanted to kiss her more.

The moment their lips met, he knew that no matter what happened in the future, he'd always love her.

She pulled away, touched his lips with her finger, then put space between them. "What about you?" she asked, her voice shaky.

He couldn't pull his thoughts together. "I beg your pardon?" All he could think about was how much he loved her.

"When we get home. What are your plans? Will you stay with the CIA?" Her forehead crinkled in a frown as he continued to watch her.

"Oh . . ." he stopped. Did he dare tell her his heart's desire? "I don't know. But to tell you the truth, I think I'm done as well."

Her surprise was easy to see. "Really?" He could almost believe she was pleased by his answer, yet she shook her head. "I can't see you doing anything but this. I figured one day you'd take over Coleman's job." She smiled.

That she thought of him only as a career agent hurt, and he struggled to keep that to himself. "Naw, I want to live in the sunlight. I'm tired of the shadows." He hesitated, then told her his dream. "My grandfather left me his spread outside Billings, Montana. Almost a thousand acres. I haven't been there in years, but after this, well . . . I can see myself getting snowed in for months on end with nothing to worry about besides how I'm going to bring in food."

She stared at him as if seeing him for the first time. "That sounds amazing. Tell me about the ranch." Her voice held a wistful note that he understood completely. They didn't know if they would walk out of here alive. The odds were against them on every turn.

"As I said, it sits on a thousand acres of pristine country. The cabin itself is small, but roomy enough. My grandfather built it for my grandmother as a wedding gift. They lived there for going on fifty years and raised two kids."

"They sound like a wonderful couple. How long have they been gone?"

Jax still missed his grandparents every day. "Grandma died about twenty years ago. Grandad lived at the cabin until his death six years ago. He taught me a lot of things about surviving, and life. He was a God-fearing man who brought me to the Lord when I was a teenager."

"Oh, Jax," she took his hand again, looping her fingers with his. "He sounds like a special man. I wish I could have met him."

He kept his focus on their joined hands. "Grandad would have liked you a lot. He'd say you had spunk." He laughed. "That's how he used to describe my grandmother."

Their eyes held. His chest grew tight. He so wanted a future with her. He could almost picture it. He and Erin living at the cabin. Raising a family together. Living in the light.

Before he could wrangle his straying thoughts, a noise in the distance captured his attention. A twig snapped beneath a footstep, and his heartrate accelerated.

Erin heard it too. With his heart racing, he leapt to his feet and grabbed his backpack. "Hurry," he whispered.

Jax grabbed her hand and together they raced through the woods as fast as they could run while he prayed they'd have enough strength to survive one more attack.

Chapter Seventeen

The world blurred around her. Erin wasn't sure how much farther she could go. She was grateful for Jax's hand around hers, his strength beside her. He wouldn't let her fall.

"Don't stop, Erin," Jax urged, his voice laced with tension. With those words still ringing in her ears, gunshots drowned out the sound of her labored breathing. Multiple gunshots. Helpless tears filled her eyes, making it impossible to see anything. She could no longer think clearly anymore. How was she supposed to fight off an army of soldiers who were intent on silencing her and Jax?

"Over there. That rock outcropping. If we can make it there, we can hold them off until we figure out our next move." Jax all but dragged her along with him, diving behind the cover of the rocks. He took out his weapon and returned fire.

The sound of gunshots so close snapped her out of her daze. She wanted to live. Wanted to see that cabin in Montana for herself. Wanted Jax forever. She grabbed her rifle and shot in the direction of their attackers. Silence followed her deluge.

"I don't hear anything. Where are they?" Jax took out the binoculars. "I don't see them."

While they both reloaded, Erin glanced behind them. She could just make out that the ground behind them sloped downward. If they could keep low enough, they had a chance to escape unnoticed by their attackers. She pointed behind them. "If we can make it down without getting shot, we might be able to get away."

"Go. I'll hold them off until you reach the valley."

Erin didn't let him finish. "I'm not leaving you behind. We do this together or not at all."

A hint of a smile touched his lips. "We do this together."

Ducking as low as possible, they started down the mountainside as fast as they could. Once they were a safe distance away, they straightened and ran.

Behind them, Erin heard more gunfire. The enemy still believed they were holed up on the mountain.

"It won't take them long before they realize we're not returning fire, and they'll come after us."

Gathering her waning strength, Erin ran as fast as she could. Jax raced beside her, his labored breathing matching hers.

They reached the bottom of the mountain that opened up into a valley where thick grass grew. "Keep going, Erin. Whatever you do, don't stop." His voice sounded winded, little more than a whisper.

Voices resounded behind them followed by gunshots. The men had stormed the place where they'd hidden and knew they weren't there any longer.

"I see them. They're getting away." That voice. There was something familiar about the man who spoke. It took everything inside of her not to look back.

She ran as hard as she could. Nothing but open space stretched out before them. There was no place to take cover. Their only chance was to outrun the men coming after them.

With hope fading inside her, she glanced at Jax. She loved him. She didn't want to lose him like this. He turned, sensing her watching him, and managed a smile. A shot splintered the night. Jax's smile turned to horror. He grabbed his leg with one hand. The other stretched out in front of him. He stumbled—tried to catch himself, but couldn't.

Erin screamed and raced for his side then knelt next to him. He'd been shot in the leg and was losing blood rapidly, but there wasn't time to tie off the wound.

"No, no, no," she whispered. "We have to keep going." She saw more than a dozen men racing toward them. She wrapped her arms around his waist, trying to lift him to his feet.

"Go on without me," Jax mumbled. "Save yourself."

She shook her head. "I'm not leaving you behind." She continued to try and help him to his feet, but she wasn't strong enough. "Jax, stay with me," she said, when he closed his eyes. "We have to go." She grabbed him beneath his arms and began dragging him. It took all her strength to move him a few yards, yet she didn't stop. She wasn't leaving him behind to die. They were in this together. She'd die for him.

"Erin, please, you have to go on. I don't want you to die like this. Go. Find the evidence Blake left you and bring them to justice. I love you, Erin. I love you."

Her footsteps faltered. He loved her. Tears sprang to her eyes. Jax loved her. And she loved him. It was a bittersweet realization that might have come too late for either of them, but she had to try. Had to make him understand how much she loved him too.

Before she could get the words to come out of her mouth—tell him how she felt about him—someone ran toward her. Out of the corner of her eye, she saw an object coming her way, then something hard slammed against her temple. She dropped to her knees. Her vision grew hazy. She was kicked hard, and she fell to the ground. Her eyes weighted down. Closed. She was inches from Jax. She peered over at him and realized he'd lost consciousness. A tear slipped from her eye.

"Get them out of here." That voice! She'd been right, she did recognize the voice. Her fuzzy brain struggled to bring the name to mind. It sounded like . . .

She knew the man who ordered Jax to be hauled away. Her heart thundered against her chest. It was impossible. It couldn't be. Erin rolled onto her back, forcing her eyes open. *He* stared down at her. The world spun, and she tried to make sense of what she was seeing. It wasn't possible. It couldn't be.

"Goodbye, Erin. You should have died when it was your turn." Before she could formulate a response. The butt of a weapon struck her head again. Her eyes slammed shut. Consciousness slipped away. Her last coherent thought was nice guys couldn't always be trusted.

* * *

His eyes felt glued in place. Jax struggled to open them. The tiniest movement sent searing pain up his leg. He'd been shot. Where was he? He remembered running from the enemy and then . . . Erin!

Jax forced his eyes open. Nothing but darkness surrounded him. He felt around and realized he was lying on a dirt floor. He tried to stand, but his injured leg wouldn't allow it.

"Erin, are you here?" he called out because he had to know. Silence followed. He somehow managed to pull himself up using only one leg.

Where was she? He had to find her. Standing upright, his head touched the roof. Using one leg, he hopped around. Felt stone walls close. He was in a small enclosed space. He hopped around some more, then slammed into something and stumbled to the ground.

Someone moaned. Erin. He felt around until he found her. She was lying on the floor. She wasn't moving.

Jax shook her hard, and she moaned again. "Erin, wake up."

"Jax? Thank God, you're alive." She sounded so weak, her voice barely audible.

"I'm right here with you," he told her, trying to keep the panic from his tone.

"What happened?" she asked and then gasped, and he knew something bad was coming. "Oh Jax, I know who's behind this." The terror in her voice had his full attention.

"What do you mean?" Before she could answer, the door flew open, slamming against the opposing wall.

Jax swiveled toward the sound, blinding light forcing him to squint and shield his eyes. Several people entered the tiny space. It took a few seconds for his eyes to adjust to the light.

When he could see clearly, he stared in horror at the person standing before him. It was impossible. He was seeing things. He blinked, then blinked again, but the image remained the same.

"Peter? But . . . I thought . . ." Peter smiled as realization finally began to dawn. He was nothing like the man he considered a friend. The person standing before him had never been his friend. Peter was the one behind the attack that killed all their men and the one who killed Blake. Peter was the mastermind behind the heroin smuggling, not Coleman.

Next to Peter, Kabir stood guard, along with four other men whom Jax didn't recognize.

"So, you figured it out," Peter finally spoke. "Well, it was only a matter of time. Not that it matters now. You two aren't going to walk out of here."

Beside him, Erin managed a sitting position, edging closer to Jax.

"Why?" was the only question Jax could formulate.

Peter scoffed at the question. "Why do you think? The money. It's always been about the money. And we had the perfect setup. We smuggled the heroin out of the country with the help of Ahmed Sediqi, the Afghan ambassador's driver. He made sure no one from the embassy caught on to what we were doing and the ambassador stayed in the dark." Peter stopped, his expression distasteful. "Then Blake grew a conscience. Wanted out. I told him to keep his mouth shut and everything would be fine, but he didn't. That's why he had to die. It would have been over with Blake's death, but you couldn't let it go, could you, Jax."

Another piece of the puzzle fell into place. "You found out I was looking into Blake's death. You had Sediqi keep tabs on me and Erin because you were afraid we'd find out the truth behind Blake's death." Jax stopped as something else dawned on him. "When I went to the embassy and started asking questions, you knew the ambassador would be curious. That's why you had both him and Sediqi killed. You were afraid if Sediqi were questioned, he'd fold and tell them everything."

Peter seemed surprised. "How did you find out about that?"

"Coleman," Jax said and couldn't believe they'd thought Coleman responsible for Peter's crimes. "You almost had me convinced he was behind this."

Peter's expression turned cold. "Well, it doesn't matter. You two will be dead soon enough. The 'real traitors' will die. Al Hasan will be branded a terrorist responsible for bringing in illegal arms into Afghanistan, and Coleman will be dubbed incompetent."

"And you and Kabir will become heroes," Erin finished for him.

Peter's mouth curled into a smile. "That's right. I'll probably get a medal. Maybe even Coleman's job."

"Why'd you frame Al Hasan?" Jax asked because he had to know. If they were going to die here, he wanted to know everything.

Peter shook his head. "What choice did I have? He saw my face several years back. I was talking to Blake's asset, a man by the name of Ghaazi Niazai. Ghaazi was one of Al Hasan's men that I'd recruited to work for me. Ghaazi provided the safest routes to move the heroin out of the country and the weapons back into Afghanistan. One day, when I was meeting with Ghaazi, Al Hasan saw me. Even though Ghaazi said he'd smoothed things over with Al Hasan, I knew it was only a matter of time before he figured out I was CIA. I had to find a way to eliminate Al Hasan, but I couldn't do it myself."

"So you made up the story of him being a terrorist to have the CIA do your dirty work," Erin said, revulsion in her tone.

"That's right," Peter said, unmoved by her disgust. "It would have worked, too, if you two had died when you were supposed to. I took out Ghaazi because I could no longer trust him not to spill his guts to Al Hasan for mercy. After I got rid of Blake, and you two kept digging into what happened, well, I had to act fast, so I faked the evidence that pointed to someone from your unit being a mole. Later, I set up the offshore account in Erin's name. She was the perfect target. Sam found the evidence easily enough. He brought it to my attention. Everything was working until Sam drew me aside and started asking questions. I knew then I had to take your entire unit out. It was the only way to cover my tracks."

Jax couldn't believe he was hearing this from the man he'd once considered a friend. "You won't get away with it," he insisted, without sounding convincing.

"That's where you're wrong. There's no one coming to your aid. Soon, I'll take care of you two both, and I'll emerge the hero in all of this." Peter spared them both a final glance. "I'd suggest you make your peace with God, or whatever you believe in, because I'm expecting the word to come through at any time. And then, my friend, you'll be dead."

With those parting words, Peter and the rest of his men left them alone and the room returned to darkness.

Jax reached for Erin and drew her close. If their time was almost up, he wanted her to know everything. "I love you, Erin. I've been in love with you since the moment I met you, but after losing Blake, well, I knew it was real. I love you, and I want us to live. We can't die here in this dingy hovel. We have to live and have a future . . . together." He stopped for a breath and heard her sob.

"I want that too. I love you as well, Jax. More than anything, I love you, and I want to survive this. See your cabin in Montana." She hesitated. "Grow old with you."

Jax's heart soared and he kissed her with all the love inside of him that had been waiting to take flight.

"There's not much time. There's no other way out of here except through the door, but we can't give up hope. We have to do whatever we can to keep fighting."

She nodded against his chest. "They took our weapons and phones. We'll have to use the element of surprise. Can you walk?"

He couldn't, but he wasn't going to tell her that. "I think so. You stand at one side of the door and I'll be on the other. If nothing else, we can take some of them out. We'll go down fighting. We won't give up."

Erin rose to her feet and helped him to his. With a final kiss, Jax hopped over to the left side of the door with Erin's help. Before she took her position, the outdoors erupted in gunfire.

She clutched his arms. "What's happening?"

He shook his head. "I don't know." The gunfight continued for a long time, peppered with screams. It sounded like a war zone outside, and they were locked in a small cell unable to decide their own fate.

With his thoughts reeling, he heard a key slip into the door's lock. Erin raced to the opposite side, flattening herself against the stone wall. The door opened slowly. It was now or never. Jax charged the first man inside, taking his opponent by surprise. They both hit the ground hard. Jax screamed in pain as he landed on his injured leg and quickly lost control of the battle.

Erin raced to his aid. Before she could land a punch, the man spoke, taking them both by surprise.

"Enough. I'm here to help you, not fight you." Al Hasan!

Relief swept through him. It wasn't Peter and his thugs after all. They were saved.

"What's happening out there," Jax managed when he was able to right himself.

"Well, it looks as if I saved your lives again." Jax didn't miss the humor in Al Hasan's voice, but it was okay. It was more than okay, it was fantastic.

"It does at that, and, boy, are we grateful," he said with a chuckle.

Al Hasan spotted Jax's wounded leg. "You're hurt. Your people are here. I'll get one of them to assist you." *Your people are here?* Jax had no idea what he was talking about.

"I'll be fine. I want out of here."

Al Hasan put his arm around Jax's waist, and Erin did the same. Together, they helped him out into the bright sunlight.

Jax glanced around. Just outside was a small Christian church and a cemetery. The building where they'd been held prisoner had once been some type of storage for tools. Now, they stood on hallowed ground while chaos surrounded them. A battle had been fought there, yet he and Erin had survived. God had seen them through, and Jax would be forever thankful.

"There's Coleman," Erin said, surprised. Jax spotted the director coming their way.

"I'm happy to see you two alive," Coleman said, shaking both their hands.

"Not as glad as we are to see you," Jax said. "Where's Peter?"

Coleman shook his head. "He didn't make it. We captured a few of his men, Kabir included, but the others died. This is one bad thing," Coleman murmured.

A medic came over to Jax to treat his wound. They'd bandage his leg now and remove the bullet stateside.

He sought out Erin, who stood by Coleman's side. Her head was covered in blood and she held onto her side.

"She needs attention right way," Jax told the medic once the guy had finished bandaging his leg.

"I'm okay," she murmured.

"No, you're not. Let him help you, Erin. I don't want anything to happen to you," Jax said, and she relented.

Once they were both looked after, Coleman returned, surveying the activity around them. "It's going to take months to untangle the full extent of Peter's treason." Disgust tinged Coleman's tone.

Jax shook his head. He couldn't believe the man he'd considered a friend and trusted with his life—with his team members' lives—was dirty all along.

"How's your friend the ambassador?" Jax asked.

Coleman's mouth tightened into a grim line. "He will be okay, but he was very lucky. His driver has been taken into custody. He's part of this as well. I've asked Ambassador Nuristani to allow us access to him. Hopefully, we can glean some useful information from him. I'll need you both on this. There's more out there than what we've discovered so far. This is the tip of the iceberg."

Jax glanced at Erin. She smiled and pointed up at the sun. He took her hand and pulled her close.

"If it's all the same to you, Coleman, I think we're done with this world. It almost cost us both our lives. We lost too many friends to Peter's greed. But we survived, and Erin and I want to make the most of the second chance we've been given. We want to live in the light from here on out. No more darkness."

Epilogue

One month later, outside Billings, Montana

"Well, what do you think?" Jax asked as he carried her over the threshold of the cabin, their new home, then set her on her feet.

Erin glanced around, her eyes shining. "It's beautiful. Oh, Jax, it's beautiful." And it was. The drive up to the cabin was like something out of a postcard. Breathtaking mountain views, covered in snow. The scent of pine and spruce trees tantalized her senses. She was in love, and she hadn't even seen the cabin . . . until now.

"I love it." She turned to him and threw her arms around him. "And I love you too."

They'd gotten married the second they could arrange the ceremony at the small church where Jax attended. The service was simple. Only a few close friends in attendance. They'd left for Montana soon after. It was hard to believe the deadly world they'd survived in for so long was finally finished for them. Even though she knew it to be true, Erin still found herself looking over her shoulder, expecting something from the past to reach out and snatch away her happiness. Somewhere near Montana she finally managed to relax, thanks to the man seated by her side who held her hand most of the way.

Now, as she stared at her new home, the future had never looked brighter. The sun was shining on them, but there was still one thing left to do. She had to do it for Blake.

"I know the perfect place," Jax said, as if reading her thoughts. "There's this spot not too far from here. In the springtime, there are flowers everywhere. I think Blake would like it there."

She smiled. God had blessed them with a second chance at life. When she thought about how close to death they'd both come, Erin knew they owed their lives to God's mercy and sovereignty. He'd sent a suspected terrorist as an angel of light to rescue them more than a few times. Only God could come up with a plan like that.

Then there was Jax. She'd be grateful every day for their life together. She loved him with all her heart. There'd be no more shadows for them. They'd survived to enjoy the sunlight and whatever adventure God brought their way. With Jax's help, she would do everything in her power to be grateful each day of what was left of her life and to love the man at her side with all her heart. Because they'd finally found their sunlight, and she wasn't about to go back to the darkness ever again.

THE COST OF REDEMPTION

SERIES

Book 1 – Hallowed Ground

Book 2 – Sacred Cause – Coming April 2020

Book 3 – Consecrated Sacrifice – Coming Fall 2020

Book 4 – Silent Night – Coming Christmas 2020

Be the first to know when Mary Alford's next book is available!

Follow her at https://www.bookbub.com/authors/mary-alford to get

an alert whenever she has a new release, preorder, or discount!

Also by Mary Alford

Summer of Suspense – A USA Today Bestselling Anthology that includes Storm Warnings, the prequel to Mary's Courage Under Fire Series

Distant Thunder (The Prequel to Storm Warning) – October 2019

Strike Force – Book one of Courage Under Fire Series – Coming December 2019

And Coming in 2020

Zero Visibility – February 2020

Thin Ice – March 2020

Chinook Winds – May 2020

The Chill of an Early Fall – Book One of Amish Country Secrets – Coming November 2019

Winter's First Frost – January 2020

From Love Inspired Suspense

Amish Country Kidnapping – Coming January 2020

Amish Country Murder – Coming March 2020

Grave Peril - A Scorpion Team Series

Standoff At Midnight Mountain – A Scorpion Team Series

Framed For Murder – A Scorpion Team Series

Deadly Memories – A Scorpion Team Series

Rocky Mountain Pursuit – A Scorpion Team Series

Forgotten Past

From Forget Me Not Romances

An Autumn Chill

Christmas at Cedar Creek

Amish Christmas Wishes

Past Sins

Eye of The Storm

Layers of The Truth

Nowhere to Run – Love On The Run Series

In Plain Sight – Covert Justice Series

Saving Agent Tanner – Covert Justice Series

Every Beat – Covert Justice Series

For a full list of Mary Alford's books, visit

www.MaryAlford.net.

About Mary Alford

USA TODAY Best-Selling Author Mary Alford loves giving her readers the unexpected. Combining unforgettable characters with unpredictable plots that result in novels the reader will not want to put down.

Her titles have appeared on the USA TODAY BESTSELLERS list, the PUBLISHER'S WEEKLY BESTSELLERS list, and have finaled in the Daphne du Maurier award of excellence in mystery, the Beverly, the Maggie, and the Selah Awards.

In addition to being a writer, Mary is an avid reader. She loves to cook, can't face the day without coffee, and her three granddaughters are the apple of her eye. She and her husband live in the heart of Texas in the middle of seventy acres, with two cats and one dog.

Mary is very active online and would love to connect with readers on:

Facebook: www.facebook.com/maryalfordauthor

Twitter: https://twitter.com/maryalford13

Instagram: https://www.instagram.com/maryjalfordauthor

Or any of the social media platforms listed at www.maryalford.net.

Made in the
USA
Monee, IL